ERNEST H. GABRIELSON

CANDI'S *Journey*

iUniverse, Inc.
Bloomington

Candi's Journey

Copyright © 2012 Ernest H. Gabrielson

iUniverse books may be ordered through booksellers or by contacting:

iUniverse
1663 Liberty Drive
Bloomington, IN 47403
www.iuniverse.com
1-800-Authors (1-800-288-4677)

ISBN: 978-1-4759-3561-5 (sc)
ISBN: 978-1-4759-3562-2 (e)

Printed in the United States of America

iUniverse rev. date: 10/17/2012

Acknowledgements and Dedication

Candi's Journey is completely a work of fiction. While I had some experience in the Marine Corps and the classroom, I have very little knowledge of any of the training procedures or activities of any law enforcement organization. When the fictional Pima County Sheriff's department is used, those activities are wholly imaginary, and any resemblance to the real thing is coincidental.

This book is respectfully dedicated to Sheriff Dupnik and the men and women of the Pima County Sheriff's Department. Members of that organization were extremely helpful to me as I imagined my characters wearing that uniform proudly.

This book could not have been written without the able editing of Jacque Wallace.

CHAPTER 1

—◆—

"CANDI, I'M GLAD YOU CAME in early. Colonel Kincaide called a few minutes ago and wants you to report at 1300."

Lieutenant Candi Adams got a worried look on her pretty face as she replied, "Oh, my God! I'll bet that he found out that I let Roy Caldwell off the hook last night."

"How was that, Candi?" asked Captain Richards. "Do you really think the Colonel is angry about that? I'll bet he doesn't even care about it. Caldwell and he served together at Paris Island, and he knows what a hothead Caldwell can be after a few drinks."

Candi managed a smile, "He was hauled in slightly drunk and a bit belligerent. His wife is dying of cancer, and I guess he needed to have a little something to take his mind off his trouble; but he didn't have to beat up a sailor who made a little fun of the Corps. I told him to go straight back to his area and stay there. I hope that he did that without another fight. He's such a good Marine that we have to cut him some slack. Besides he has a Purple Heart along with his Silver Star."

Ted Richards smiled, "I know the Colonel doesn't want to see you about him. It's probably about your letter requesting to go inactive. I'll bet he thinks he can change your mind. Don't forget how intimidating he is. There's a lot of Marines tougher than you who are terrified of him. Try to stand up to him."

"Well, I'm going to face him bravely, regardless of what he wants. At least I hope I don't turn *chicken* in his office. Sometimes I think he has only one mood—angry."

Just before 1300, Candi entered Colonel Kincaide's office. "Hi, Sergeant Michaels. Will you tell the Colonel that Lieutenant Adams is reporting as ordered? He said he wanted to see me this afternoon at 1300." She smiled at him conspiratorially and whispered, "Do you have an idea what it's about? I'd like a little preparation time."

"No, I don't Lieutenant, but he's been on a tear all morning. He's on the phone right now." The sergeant pointed across the room and added, "There's lots of reading material by the chairs. I'll let you know when he'll see you. Have a seat, please."

Candi walked over to a row of straight-back chairs, picked up a copy of the <u>Leatherneck</u> magazine, and sat down. Since Colonel Kincaide was an old, grizzled warrior with a booming voice, Candi, a young lieutenant, was a little terrified of him. *Being called into Kincaide's office is a lot worse than being called into the principal's office in high school.*

"Lieutenant, the Colonel will see you now. Follow me."

Sergeant Michaels opened the door after knocking and held the door open for Candi. "Lieutenant Adams, reporting as ordered, Sir," Candi said as she entered and stood at attention before the colonel's beautiful walnut desk. The office had many framed photos—all showing Marines in battle. They ranged through many eras—WWI, WW2, Korea, Vietnam and now Iraq and Afghanistan.

Kincaide looked up from reading a paper, "Sit down, Lieutenant. Can I get you a cup of coffee?"

Surprised by his calm, soft voice, Candi replied, "No, thank you, Sir. I just finished lunch."

The Colonel rose from his chair and came around the desk to sit on one of the chairs in front of his desk next to Candi. "Candace," he hesitated and then asked, "May I call you Candace, Lieutenant?"

"Yes, Sir, but my friends call me Candi." His soft manner was so unexpected that Candi now began to tremble.

"Thank you, Candi. Captain Richards speaks highly of you. Your work in base security is first rate."

Totally surprised and now alarmed by his soft voice and kindly manner, Candi tried not to be intimidated by his many rows of ribbons and battle stars. "I hope this isn't about Sergeant Caldwell, Sir. He's going through a hard time now, and the corpsman he decked isn't hurt. I just hope he didn't get in trouble after he left me."

"No, Candi. I'm aware of Sergeant Caldwell's trouble last night. He's a fine Marine." Kincaide reached out and grabbed

Candi's small pretty hands in his gnarled large ones. "Candi, I called you in because I know that you're friendly with Gunny Mitchell."

Now I know why I'm here. He's found out about us. "Yes, Sir, Gunny Mitchell and I are acquaintances." *I hope that's all he knows about us.*

"Candi, I have some terrible news for you. Gunny Sergeant Mitchell was killed this morning in a helicopter accident near Barstow."

The Colonel felt Candi's fingers tighten within his grip even before her face showed any emotion. Then suddenly her face crumbled as tears gushed down her cheeks. "Colonel, are you sure? Can it be a mistake? Please, Sir..."

"Candi, I've spent the morning on this. All six of the crew were killed. Jim Mitchell was positively identified."

Through her sobbing and tears, she managed to say in a voice that was almost a whisper, "We were getting married in two weeks. Jim and I were going to Arizona this weekend so he could meet my folks. I know I'll be court-martialed and given a bad conduct discharge. Now I don't really care, Sir. I don't know what I'm going to do now."

For the first time since they started talking, the Colonel managed a small smile. He reached up and put his hand under her chin and lifted her head up to face him. "Candi, you've done nothing wrong. We've known about your friendship with Jim Mitchell for about a year. I know that you were careful to be discreet about being together, but believe me you did nothing wrong. Jim talked about you with General Wingate and me. The General thought that it was a good idea for Jim to date you after he returned from overseas because we thought it would add to his cover story. However, we didn't know that you were going to get married. Both General Wingate and I discussed your devotion to each other with Mitchell. He told us how much he loved you many times.

Now there's something you probably didn't know about Jim. He was not a platoon sergeant in a line company, but he was proud of the fact that he was going into action with Echo Company in the 2nd Battalion. That also added something to his cover story."

"Sir…" Candi interrupted. "He went overseas with Echo Company as a platoon sergeant."

"More cover, Candi. He was sent to the Mid-East to discover who was selling our weapons to the wrong people, and we felt that an enlisted man could do the job better than an officer. He did the job well, and a few supply people are up for a general court-martial. When he returned to the states, he requested that he remain undercover, while continuing to see you. Both General Wingate and I knew that wasn't the real reason he wanted to 'break regulations.' That's when he told the general and me that he adored you."

While sitting perfectly still, Candi's small hands began rubbing the Colonel's hands unconsciously.

"Let me get you a tissue." Kincaide got up and took several tissues from a box on his desk and handed them to her. He sat down and again reached for her hand. She appeared to be in such agony that he wanted to hold her as a father might.

"I know this is inappropriate, but, Sir, I think I'm going to faint." Her eyes closed and she would have slipped off the chair had the colonel not grabbed her. He pulled her close against his chest. She continued to remain there as she whispered, "Please, Sir, tell me what to do now. I'm so confused."

"I'll prepare leave papers for you. You need some time to grieve, and you should go home for awhile. You live in Arizona according to Sergeant Michaels."

She raised her head and pulled away from his embrace just a small bit. "I'm sorry, Sir. I guess I'm not much of a Marine if I faint."

"That's quite understandable under the circumstances."

"Jim was so proud that he was a Marine."

The Colonel replied, "Yes, he was, and he was a credit to the Corps. He will receive the Navy Cross and be buried at Arlington, if his folks approve."

"Thank you, Sir. I know it would make him proud to be buried with so many of his nation's bravest heroes."

"I would like you, Lieutenant Adams, to lead his honor guard. Do you think you're up to that?"

"Yes, Sir. I must be there when his mother is presented with the flag."

She stood up and said, "You must be extremely busy, Colonel. I'll leave, but I want to thank you for your kindness and concern for me."

Kincaide walked her to the door while saying, "I'm sorry, Candi, that I was the one that had to tell you the horrible news."

"Sir, I know that has to be one of your hardest tasks." She walked slowly through the ante-room and out into the sunshine of Camp Pendleton.

I wish it were a cloudy day to match my dismal mood. Standing on the steps of Colonel Kincaide's office facing the sun, she longed for someone to tell her what she should do now. Officers and enlisted personnel walked past her, and probably most wanted to know why an officer was just standing still with tears streaming down her cheeks. When she managed to hold her sobbing in check, she wiped her eyes and headed for the officer's club. *Maybe a drink might help. Maybe Caldwell and I can get together and cry for his dying wife and the love of my life.* When she entered the club, she saw it wasn't very crowded at this time of day. For that, she was thankful since she didn't want to talk to anyone for awhile.

"What'll you have, Lieutenant? Your usual?" Sergeant Tim Monahan was behind the bar waiting for her to speak.

"A brandy and soda, Tim. I'll be at the table over there," Candi replied as she walked away before he could ask her any questions.

Monahan knew something was terribly wrong with Candi because she was usually a very happy and upbeat person. She was happier still when she was away from Pendleton and Oceanside with Jim Mitchell. When he brought the drink over to her table, he said, "That's on me, Lieutenant. It's almost a double. You look like you need it."

She nodded and smiled briefly at him while putting both hands around the drink. From time to time, Tim looked over to her noting that she hadn't even sipped at the drink but just stared at nothing.

"Gimme a cold beer, Sarge," Lieutenant Peck said, drawing Tim away from his concern about Candi momentarily.

After passing Peck his beer and giving him his change, Tim hoped that he would leave Candi alone, but that was not to be.

Peck marched over and sat down opposite Candi. "Please go away, Fred. I don't want any company right now." She didn't look at him as she continued to hold her head down.

"Come on, Babe. Lighten up. This is payday and the start of the weekend. Where's your sergeant boyfriend today?" He asked this in a sardonic manner.

"Leave me alone," Candi said in a low voice tinged with anger. When he still didn't leave, she raised her voice, "GO AWAY. I DON'T WANT ANY COMPANY, ESPECIALLY YOU!"

"I can take a hint, Candi. You don't have to shout."

"Go to hell, Fred. But do it now, please."

When Lieutenant Peck finally got up and moved away, he wandered over to the juke box and stood in front of it for a long time drinking his beer and trying to figure out why Candi snapped at him. He turned away without coming to any conclusion and walked back to the bar. He noticed Monahan was talking to the clerk from the colonel's office. "Hey, Sergeant, gimme another beer. This one leaked away." He chuckled at his own lame joke.

When Monahan drew him another beer, Peck said, "What's the matter with Lieutenant Adams, Sarge? Did she catch her boyfriend in bed with someone else?"

Monahan turned red with anger, "Lieutenant, if I wasn't enlisted and you weren't an officer, I'd beat the shit out of you." After a slight pause, he added, "Gunny Mitchell was killed this morning. Now I'm busy, so drink your beer and shut the fuck up!"

CHAPTER 2

———◆———

Surprised by Monahan's angry outburst and realizing at the same time that his remark was definitely out of line, Peck turned to leave, not even finishing his beer. "Sorry, Sarge, I was out of line. I didn't know that Jim was killed today."

"That's okay, Lieutenant. I just found out about it myself, and I kinda lost my head. Sorry."

When Peck walked by Candi's table, he touched her shoulder and said, "Sorry about Jim. He was a very nice guy and a good Marine." He left the room without looking again at the stricken woman.

Finally, Candi took a few sips from her drink. Tim noticed and, without even thinking about it, mixed another and took it to her table. She looked up at him as he took the first glass away. "Thanks, Tim." She forced a faint smile as she picked up the fresh drink.

Candi was lost in her memories of him. *He was so wonderful. We could've been very happy together.*

She had first met Jim about a year earlier. Her first sight of him was certainly not very impressive. He was dragged into her office by a pair of MPs. He was as drunk as it gets, but he attempted to stand at attention in his disheveled uniform facing her. "Sorry about this, Ma'am. I don't know why I took a couple of extra drinks tonight. I hope you believe me when I say that I hardly ever do that. I guess I was celebrating the fact that Echo Company is leaving for the Gulf next week. I hope you don't put this on my record, Ma'am. I'd hate to lose a stripe just before we ship out." He smiled at her and said, "I promise that this won't happen again, Ma'am. Please accept my word on that."

The two MPs who brought him in shook their heads and smiled as they left the office.

He sure has a winning smile, she thought and then said in a school teacherish voice, "Sergeant, I'm surprised that a gunny like you doesn't confine your drinking to the base. I'm sure you know better. Being drunk and fighting in Oceanside doesn't speak well of the Corps."

"I do, Ma'am. I promise I'll never do it again if you'll let it slide this time. I'll do anything you ask if you don't report this to my company commander. He takes a dim view of drunkenness in uniform. He says, 'Get drunk, but don't get the uniform drunk.'"

Smiling inwardly, Candi said, "Sergeant Mitchell, did you mean it when you said that you'd do anything if I don't make a written report of this incident?"

"Yes, Ma'am. I'm pleading with…"

"Never mind the pleading, Sergeant. Just go over to that chair in the corner and drink a cup or two of coffee. When you think you're able to walk straight, I'll drive you to your area because I don't believe that you could get there by yourself. Which battalion do you belong to?"

"Second battalion, Fifth Marines, Ma'am. I'm the section chief of a mortar platoon in a line company."

Something in his smile and apparent sincerity rang a bell with her. He was a big, good-looking fellow but good looking only in a rough sort of way. He was probably 24 or 25 and had been in the Corps long enough to have earned his rank and a four-year hash mark. After thanking her and leaving her desk, he sat quietly in the chair drinking coffee and smiling at her when she looked at him.

When her relief came, she went over and asked, "Are you ready to go, Sergeant? Do you think now you can walk like a Marine sergeant should?"

"Yes, Ma'am, but you don't have to…"

"Let's go, Sergeant. I don't trust you to go back to your barracks alone tonight."

Jim said as they got in the jeep, "I really appreciate this, Ma'am. I'll pay you back if I can do anything for you.

Lieutenant, may I ask what your name is? I can't read your name tag in the dark."

"I'm Candace Adams, but you call me Lieutenant Adams, please. No first names, Sergeant."

He grabbed her right arm and said, "I think you're the

nicest and most beautiful Marine in the whole history of the Corps."

"Thanks, Sergeant, but that's a bit of an exaggeration. It's BS, but some women like to hear some BS occasionally." He sat quietly while looking at her. "But please don't try your BS on me. It won't work." After a few more minutes passed, they arrived in his company area.

"Here's your area. Good luck when you ship out. Please come back safely. And, please, be a little smarter when you drink. If it comes to my attention that you have done this again, I'll surely have to report it, and you'll probably lose a stripe. Don't let that happen and remember the promise you made to me."

"I'll buy you a drink when I get back," he said and then hesitated before adding, "Candi is a beautiful name and you're a beautiful girl." After saying this, Jim turned on his heel and hurried away before she could bawl him out for using her nickname and not saluting her.

The next day, when she got off duty, she saw him standing in the shadows across the street from her office. She smiled to herself as she caught him following her jeep. He was running to keep her in sight. When she finished shopping at the PX, he *accidentally* came up behind her as she was paying for her purchases.

"Hello, Lieutenant. Fancy meeting you here."

"Yes, it's quite a coincidence, isn't it, Sergeant? Do you

need a ride back to your area today? You look a little out of breath," she asked smiling.

"I'd appreciate that, Ma'am, if it won't take you out of your way. Let me carry your packages." He took the bag from her and grabbed her arm as they went out of the PX.

On the way to his area, he sat quietly for a few minutes and then abruptly asked, "Would you please go to dinner with me tomorrow night? I think that we're being deployed very soon."

She laughed and said, "You know I can't, Sergeant, and you should know better than to ask."

"Please, Ma'am. We can wear civvies, and no one will know. We can sort of just meet accidentally like we did today, can't we?" As he asked, he looked at her pleadingly.

This time she laughed and put her hand on his arm. "I can't go to dinner with you, Sergeant, but if you happen to be at Chico's at around 1800, we might *accidentally* run into each other like we did in the PX." After she said that, she regretted it immediately. She knew how the Corps felt about an officer becoming friendly with enlisted personnel. She knew that she had made a horrible mistake but didn't know how to get out of the dilemma which she had just put herself in.

In spite of her guilty feelings, the next evening she dressed in civilian clothes and drove to the restaurant located several miles from Oceanside. When she entered, she saw that he had arrived before her and arranged for a table for two in the darkest part of the restaurant. When she approached the table, he stood and said, "My God! Ma'am, you look stunning!" As he helped her sit down, he said, "That dress takes my breath away. You're so lovely that it's even hard for me to swallow."

She laughed and said, "More BS, Sergeant? You've taken that to an art form."

During and after the meal of delicious Mexican food, they talked about a lot of things such as hometowns, school days, and early days in the Corps. She began to love his humor and intelligence, and he began to just love her. They talked for over two hours, and both were reluctant to get up. Not being able to stop himself, he held her hands while they finished talking and once brought them to his lips and kissed both hands.

When they got to the parking lot and she stood at the door of her private car, he said, "Candace, will you write to me when I go? Just a note or two once in awhile, that's all I'm asking for."

She hardly noticed it, but somehow now it almost felt right for him to call her by her first name. She went into her purse and pulled out a card and handed it to him. "I want regular reports from you, Sergeant Mitchell. I want to be sure you're safe, and I promise to do my best to answer them."

Suddenly, he grabbed her and pulled her against him. "That was the best dinner I ever had," he whispered as he nuzzled her hair.

Before pulling away quickly, she reached up and kissed

him lightly on the cheek. "Please take care, Marine. We'll have dinner again if you want when you come back."

"If I want? That's a laugh. I'll dream about that dinner the whole time I'm in the Gulf."

With twinkling eyes and a soft laugh, she replied, "Please don't dream about that when you should be keeping your head down."

"Do you know, Ma'am, that tonight is the first time I've ever been kissed by an officer, and it was wonderful? Now, with or without your permission, Lieutenant, I'm, going to kiss an officer for the first time." Before she could say "no," or pull away, he came across the space between them and kissed her softly at first and then more fervently.

"Wow, I hope that you don't kiss any other lieutenants like that, Sergeant."

"Don't worry about that. You're the only one I ever fell in love with. When I look at your face, I can't help thinking of a line of poetry we studied in high school."

She chuckled and asked, "What was the line, Jim?" His first name came to her lips almost as if they'd been of equal rank, and again she had a guilty feeling.

"Man's reach must exceed his grasp, or what's a heaven for?"

She chuckled, "My, my! A big, tough Marine who likes poetry. I think you're very unusual, Sergeant."

Turning very serious, he said, "I know you're in a league above me, but I'm going to reach out for you anyhow."

"Now, Sarge, that sounds like another line to me." She grinned trying to take the seriousness out of his declarations.

"It isn't a line at all, Candi. Because of you, I don't want to leave the States right now. Please try to keep me in mind while I'm gone." Again he looked into her soft green eyes pleadingly.

She laughed again. "Don't worry, Jim. I'll be here when you return, but make damn sure you do return. You're now kind of important to me." She hoped he didn't read too much into what she had just said.

"Okay. Now may I request something from the lieutenant?" Jim reached out and brought her face very close to him. "I'll have the image of you with me always, but could you have a picture of you on your desk tomorrow?" He smiled and added, "If you do, I'll just saunter by your office and kinda liberate it." He grinned at her when he said he'd *liberate* her picture.

She hugged him and laughed, "It won't be one where I'm in a bathing suit, but I'll bring one down for you to *accidentally* liberate, and it will fit nicely into your wallet. It'll be my college graduation picture, so it'll be about two years old. I probably had fewer wrinkles then."

As she drove away, she thought, *I could grow to love that man. Please, God, keep him safe. And please forgive me for doing something forbidden by the Corps.* In spite of her misgivings on that score, she found that she was happy that she had met him and had dinner with him. *Isn't it just my luck to find someone that might actually be THE ONE, but, of course, he's one I can never allow to come into my life. I hope that I don't start dreaming about him tonight.*

She knew that she was almost glad he was going overseas, so both of them would have a chance to think more clearly about the possibility of a relationship.

Snapped from her memories, she looked up as Tim approached her table.

CHAPTER 3

—⋅—

THE THIRD TIME TIM MONAHAN brought her a fresh drink because the ice had melted in her neglected one, Candi shook her head and said, "Thanks, Tim, but please don't bother. I just want to sit here awhile. Is that okay?" She gave him a faint smile and put her hand on his for a moment.

"It sure is, Lieutenant. But let me know if you need anything. I'm sorry about what happened to Gunny Mitchell. He and I were buddies for a long time."

In a few minutes, Lieutenants Stetson and Blogovich came in and spotted Candi. Both came over and sat in the empty chairs at her table. "We heard about the accident, and we became worried. When Georgia came to work instead of you, we knew something had happened; so we went to your apartment looking for you, and finally we came here." Betty Stetson spoke as she reached out putting her hand over Candi's.

"He's dead, Betty."

"We know. The news is all over the base," Shirley whispered as she, too, began to weep.

"Colonel Kincaide told me. He relieved me and is having Georgia fill in for me. Now I'm going with Jim's mother and the honor guard to Arlington." After she said this, tears again started down her cheeks. "He's being buried there because of his Purple Heart and Silver Star."

Both women, Betty and Shirley, took one of her hands and joined her in silence as they each squeezed a hand. All three of them were now teary eyed.

After a few minutes, Shirley broke the silence. "Are you on leave after the funeral? You should take one because going home will help."

"That's what the Colonel said. I think I'll resign my commission though. There are too many things here that remind me of him, but right now, I'm so angry at the world I can't think straight. I don't give a damn about anything."

Since both her friends knew of her secret relationship with Jim, they could talk freely with her about her relationship with an enlisted man.

"What happened? Did the Colonel tell you?" Shirley asked.

"Yes, he did. It was a helicopter accident this morning near Barstow. And he told me that Jim wasn't a gunny. He was working undercover and was actually a major."

"All the time you were with him, he didn't tell you that?" Betty asked incredulously.

"No, but he did say last night that he was going to tell me something important about himself. I thought it might be a divorce thing from his past or something like that. I guess he was going to tell me about being an officer."

Shirley said, "Let's get out of here. You need to go home and we'll go with you." Both Betty and Shirley got up and pressed Candi to get up also.

"I've been here long enough. You're right. I've got to go back to Arizona for awhile so I can think things through and make some decisions about my future."

Shirley asked, "Do you want us to stay with you, Candi? You shouldn't be alone this afternoon. We want to be with you. Now come with us, and we'll fix some dinner."

"Thanks, girls, but I need to be alone for awhile, and I'm not a bit hungry and probably nothing will stay down anyway. I've got to start thinking about what to do next."

"Okay, Candi, but we'll stop for a bite on our way. Remember that I'll be next door if you need anything," Betty said. "I don't care how late it is, please call me."

When the two women left her alone after forcing her to eat a few bites of a hamburger, she poured a glass of iced tea and took it out on her small porch and began remembering.

She remembered waving as the 2nd Battalion left the area and was surprised that she had a terrible feeling of regret because he was leaving. When the last of the trucks were out of sight, she just stood there wishing he was next to her. She felt like a balloon that's been popped, and she was sick with worry knowing what might happen to him and all the other young Marines.

Everyday she rushed home to look hurriedly through her mail hoping to find a letter from him. About a month after he left, she received her first letter which she read with a beating heart. The battalion had arrived in the Gulf, and all was well. He told her how much he missed her and that the dinner they had promised each other was going to be a private banquet with all the trimmings. He wrote, "We have so much free time that I spend a lot of it in the sack dreaming about you sitting across from me at our first dinner."

During the months he was gone, she received two phone calls from him and many letters and e-mails. They were filled with amusing anecdotes that made her smile. She answered his letters faithfully and confessed in each one that she missed him and yearned for his safe return.

When the battalion was due home, she waited in a civilian dress a little way from the crowd that was gathered to welcome sons and husbands home. She watched the happy throng as the men in the battalion jumped out of trucks and went through the crowd of civilians looking for their loved ones. Then she saw him at the edge of the milling throng looking all around. Her wondering whether he would recognize her was put to rest when she saw him running toward her carrying his duffle bag over his shoulder. He dropped the duffle and picked her up twirling her around before stopping to give her a long and passionate kiss. She loved having his arms around her and looking into his twinkling eyes and seeing his happy grin. Soon they were on their way to San Diego to have "the dinner." Half way there he pulled her car to the side of the road and threatened not to go any further until she slid over next to him. "I want you near me, so I can smell your perfume. It's been too long since I did that."

She smiled when she remembered how he had insisted that their table was to be set up just so. There was candlelight and sparkling wine. *It was sitting across from him when I discovered I loved him and didn't want him ever to go away again. I never even pretended to argue when we drove to a hotel and registered for the night as man and wife.*

In the weeks following his return, they spent every weekend together. Those weeks were the happiest ones in her life. To be discreet, they met in either San Diego or Long Beach—places far enough from Oceanside so their meetings wouldn't be discovered.

One night, however, while they were eating dinner at a posh hotel in Long Beach, Sergeant Monahan, the bartender at the Officer's Club, walked by their table and recognized both of them.

"Hi, Lieutenant Adams. It's nice to see you and Jim here." He shook Jim's hand while remarking that they had danced beautifully together.

Too frightened to pay attention to what passed between Jim and Monahan, she just gripped her wine glass imagining that their rendezvous would be the talk of Camp Pendleton in a few days. When Sergeant Monahan walked away, Jim took her hands in his. "Don't worry, Dear One. Tim and I are old friends. We were in the same platoon in boot camp, and I know he won't say anything about us being together. And please try to smile and return some color to your beautiful cheeks." He laughed and added, "Tim might like to dance with you. I said that it was okay with me, but he'd have to ask you. Do you mind? He's a very nice guy and a wonderful dancer."

His confident, amused attitude toward Tim's discovery of them brought a half smile to her lips. When she nodded her willingness to dance with Monahan, Jim signaled him over to their table. "Go ahead and you folks get on the dance floor while they're playing this slow one, but, Monahan, don't step on her toes. She'll deck you if you do. I know because I almost got decked once after I did it." He laughed aloud as he glanced at both of them.

While they were dancing to an old Jerome Kern tune, he whispered, "Lieutenant, I'm glad you and Jim found each other. He's a nice guy and you deserve one like him."

"Thanks, Tim," she responded, and added, "And, Tim, please don't…"

His laughter interrupted her. "Ma'am, you're a wonderful dancer. Jim said that he loves you. I don't blame him."

The music stopped. She reached up and pressed her cheek against his. "Thanks for the dance, Tim. I'm very happy that you're one of Jim's good buddies."

24

As she sat alone on the porch, she found herself crying again. It was after midnight before she got up and went to bed.

The next two days were filled with making arrangements for the trip to Arlington. She turned away as the casket was put on board the plane by the honor guard. When the plane landed in Denver to pick up Jim's mother, both women tried to put up a brave, tear-free front; however, it was much more difficult at Arlington. When the burial was over and his mother was presented with the flag that had covered the casket, Candi couldn't stop crying. His mother looked at her and handed the flag to one of the guard. Norma Mitchell came over to her saying, "Please don't cry for him, Candi. Let's both remember only the best moments we had with him."

Sobbing into his mother's shoulder, Candi said, "I know my loss is nothing compared to yours. I only knew him for a few months, but I never loved anyone as much as I loved Jim."

"He's in good company here, Dear. We must both be brave and go on with our lives."

When she returned to Pendleton, she went to Colonel Kincaid's office. After she was admitted, she explained to him that she wanted to resign her commission.

"Are you sure, Lieutenant?" the Colonel asked. "Please consider that carefully. You're a good officer and we'd hate losing you."

"Yes, I'm almost sure, Sir. There's too much here to remind me of Jim Mitchell. I've got to get to some other place in my life."

"Take a bereavement leave. Go home and try to put things in perspective. After a month, if you still want out of the Corps, I'll—with regret—approve your return to reserve status. Meanwhile if there is anything that I or anyone else here can do for you, please ask."

"Thank you, Sir. I'll always be proud that I was in the Corps. Now if I may, I'll say goodbye to some of the friends I've made here and do as you say. I'll take a month to think about what I should do. I believe this is inappropriate, but I'm going to do it anyway." She rose and came around his desk and put her arms around him. "I know I'm leaving the Marine Corps in good hands, Sir. I know I'll miss serving with men like you." She smiled and added, "I won't tell anyone how kind you've been to me, Sir. It would probably ruin your reputation with the troops in your command, but thank you, Sir. I'll remember you always. And I hope that if I don't resign, you'll let me stay in your command."

"Don't worry about that, Lieutenant Adams. You'll always be welcome back here."

Chapter 4

——◆——

After receiving a salute from the gate sentry after he had inspected her leave papers, Candi pulled over to the side out of the traffic lanes and stopped the car. She got out and watched the smartly-dressed sentries inspect the cars as they approached the gate. *I guess I received my last salute, but maybe Colonel Kincaide was right. I'm not sure now that I want to leave the Corps. I feel just like I did when I left home for college. God, I wish I could think straight. I'm not even sure which direction I'll use to get to Prescott. Come on, girl! Get your brain into gear.*

She turned right on the Coast Highway and headed toward Los Angeles. Two hours later she was about clear of the city. Traffic was light on the freeway which allowed her to make good time. She didn't stop until she reached Blythe. Memories of Jim kept trying to intrude into her thoughts. She fought back tears while trying to focus on her future. After drinking a soda and having one bite of a tasteless sandwich, she soon crossed the line into Arizona. Yesterday she had telephoned her parents to tell them that she was coming home. She had told them about Jim's accident the day Colonel Kincaide told her, so they knew she was coming home alone.

When she reached Flagstaff, she was so tired that she could go no further. She took a motel room and went out for a lonely dinner which she only nibbled at. While it was still light enough to see things, she drove through the campus of Northern Arizona University. Watching students bundled in overcoats walking back and forth in the snow, she smiled recalling her carefree student days here and her first contact with the Marine Officer Training Program. *We had lots of fun here in January messing around in the snow.*

When she returned to the motel, she fell into a fitful sleep. Because she arose at 4:00 am, she had trouble finding a restaurant open for coffee. When she finally did find one, she stopped for a cup of bad coffee, and tried to force down an egg.

When she came to the highway that went through Sedona and Cottonwood, she decided that she had enough of the I-17 freeway travel and took the lovely drive through Oak Creek Canyon into Sedona. She pushed through that beautiful town, and by mid-morning she reached Cottonwood. Feeling the first pangs of hunger since Jim's death, she stopped there for a late breakfast at Randall's restaurant. Soon she was on her way again and reached Prescott and home before noon.

She drove carefully through familiar snow-covered neighborhoods until she reached her parents' house, but even there she felt an unexpected sadness. *I think I've traveled in a giant circle, and I'm back where I started from.*

Sensing her pain, her dad and mother greeted her warmly. After giving and receiving hugs and kisses from both parents, she unloaded her car, putting her clothes into a familiar bedroom. Then, as in the days of her childhood, all three of them sat at the kitchen table talking. She tried to explain how she felt about Jim's death but found it extremely difficult. Her parents understood and turned the conversation toward recent news of the Verde Valley and Prescott. They told her what they knew of some of her classmates in elementary and high school.

During the next few days, she visited with several life-long friends and familiarized herself with the many changes taking place in her hometown. She smiled when she went by the old courthouse and saw the veterans from Fort Whipple hospital and dorm sitting in the sun while they watched the people pass by. She knew that those old veterans loved coming to town so they could admire the pretty young girls who passed by.

"Stop wandering around town with that dour expression, dear. Go someplace where you used to have fun with your old friends," her mother advised as Candi was sitting out on the front porch with a book in her lap staring into space without even pretending to read.

Candi responded with a half smile, "I don't know, Mom. I've been here for nearly two weeks, and somehow the town doesn't seem the same. I need something to take my mind off..."

"Oh, I forgot to tell you that your friend, Pam, called yesterday. She wants you to have lunch with her today if you can. I'm sorry I forgot all about her call. She said that she's been home from Tucson for the past few days but has to go back tomorrow. She came home because her dad was in the hospital last week. Give her a call because she also probably needs cheering up. You always got along with her, didn't you?"

"Yes. We were good friends. What does she do in Tucson? Did she say?"

"No, she didn't tell me anything. She went to the University of Arizona and I think she graduated, but she stayed down there. I've seen her parents a time or two, however. They said that she's working for the sheriff's office now. She asked me if you liked it in the Marines. I didn't tell her that you're thinking of doing something else."

"I think that I'd like to have lunch with her." Candi got up, leaving her book folded on the chair, so she wouldn't lose her place and then went to the phone. In a few minutes, she returned to the porch. "I'm going out to Dewey. Pam and I are going to have lunch there."

"Enjoy yourself, dear. Tell Pam to say 'hello' to her mom for me, will you?"

When Candi stopped outside the Blue Moon Restaurant, she looked around for her friend's old Chevy but didn't see it. When she entered the restaurant, she immediately spotted Pam's flaming red hair. Pam Henry climbed out of a booth when she saw Candi. The two former high school classmates hugged each other and then set about ordering lunch.

"Your mom told me about the tragic death of your boyfriend. I'm sorry, Candi. I'll bet he was a nice guy because you never had any truck with the other kind."

"He was, Pam. I feel like I'm under water and can't get to the surface. What about you? I heard that you got married when you left the University."

Pamela laughed, "That's ancient history. We got a divorce before our first anniversary. All he seemed to care about was himself. It just didn't work out."

Candi asked, "Pam, you stayed in Tucson and began working for the sheriff's department down there my mom said. What sort of work do you do there?"

"I'm a cop—well, actually I'm a deputy sheriff."

"Do you like doing that?"

"Yeah, I like it. As the old story goes, 'Being a cop sure beats working.' Are you going to make the Marines a career? You're a lieutenant already, I hear."

"That's my problem, Pam. I don't know what I'm going to do now. I don't believe I'll stay in the Corps, though. Too many reminders of Jim Mitchell. He was a major, but worked undercover." She smiled, "like a cop."

"Candi, why don't you come to Tucson and stay with me until you decide? I live alone in a two-bedroom apartment, and I think we could have some fun together. I'm tired of always being alone. Maybe you might enroll at the U for your masters, and there are lots of fun things to do in Tucson. How about it?"

"That might be what I need. I'll think it over. How long can you stay up here? We should at least discuss my going down there further."

Pam said, "I leave in the morning. I've got to get back to work, but let me give you my card." Pam took out her wallet, fished around for a card, and as she handed one to Candi, she said, "Here. This has both my phone and cell numbers. Please come down and let me show you the town. If you don't want to camp out with me, the apartment next to mine will be empty next week. The place is in a nice part of town, close to a lot of good stuff, and a mall is close by." She smiled and added, "and it's as affordable as apartments get nowadays."

As they were leaving the restaurant, Candi asked about Pam's old Chevy. Pam laughed and replied, "See that new Dodge truck over there? That's mine, but I still miss the old Chevy."

Almost for the first time in several weeks, Candi laughed. "I remember we used to double date in the Chevy. I remember the car, but I can't remember much about the boys we dated. Those were fun times."

"And what are you driving, Miss Lieutenant?" Pam asked this looking around at the various cars in the parking lot. "You don't drive a jeep, do you?"

Candi laughed again, "No jeep. I left them at Camp Pendleton. See that Chevy over there—the green one? That's mine. It's two years old, but it still runs well and is paid for."

Pam laughed as they gave each other hugs, "Well, I hope that you and your Chevy will come to Tucson. It's only about three hours from here. If you come, please don't get pulled over for speeding. It might be me that's writing out a ticket for you, and I hate doing that to my friends."

CHAPTER 5

———◆———

WHEN CANDI ARRIVED HOME AFTER having lunch with Pam, she went out to the back yard. While sitting in one of the lawn chairs, she opened her book, but had no intention of reading it. She began to think about her options. *I only have a little leave time left. If I'm going to stay in the Corps, I know that Colonel Kincaide will give me more time if I need it to make a decision. There are good reasons why I should stay in. I've got friends there, the pay is good, and there are a lot of things I like about living in California. But Pam's invitation to come to Tucson is also attractive. I could enroll in some courses at the University and get my teaching certificate. I've got more hours from NAU than I need to teach a couple of subjects.*

The next thing that she was aware of was noticing her mother shaking her shoulder and asking her to come in and eat supper. "I'll be right in Mom. I dozed off. I guess I needed to catch up on my sleep."

"Did you enjoy your lunch with your friend this afternoon?"

"Yes, I did. She invited me to come to stay with her in Tucson. I think that I'll do that for at least a few days. It'll give me a chance to talk to someone at the University. I need to make some decisions pretty soon. Trying to make up my mind is giving me a headache."

Her mother laughed and asked, "Is it true that she's a police officer?"

"Yes, Mom. She works for the sheriff's office down there. I still don't know if I want to go back to the Marines or stay in Arizona and go into teaching."

The next morning she set off for Tucson. She had called Pam the night before to say that she would take her up on the invitation. Pam said that she was working the day shift, but to ask at the office for a key to her apartment.

When Candi arrived in Tucson, she didn't have any trouble locating the apartment complex on Speedway. Pam had left a note to make herself at home and to relax with a glass or two of iced tea.

When Pam came home and changed her clothes, they went out for dinner. After getting seated, Pam asked, "Well, Candi, have you made a decision about the Marine Corps yet?"

"Not really. I'm going to the University in the morning to see what I need to do to get a teaching certificate. If I decide to leave the Corps, I'll need a job."

They spent the rest of the evening wandering through the Park Mall window-shopping. While they were in the food court, Pam said, "I hope you decide to stay here. We could have so much fun together."

Candi responded, "I think it would be fun too. Tucson seems to be a nice place, but if I stay, I've got to get my own place. Living in the same apartment with you, I might interfere with your love life," she said with a laugh.

"Yeah, right. I go out occasionally with a few of the single deputies, but so far, I've not found one that I want to make any permanent commitment with."

The next morning, Candi went to the University employment office. She discussed her educational background with the employment counselor and found it easy to have her transcript FAXed down from NAU.

While going over her transcript, one of the employment office councilors said, "Your papers are fine, Miss Adams, but now many English teachers are out of work just because of budget cuts. I see that you have enough hours in reading instruction to qualify you as a reading specialist. There's a bit more of a demand for them than there is for English teachers. I'll call you if anything comes across my desk."

Pam was already at home when Candi came in. "And what did you find out at the University today?" she asked.

"Well, Pam, I found out that many teachers are out of work because of budget problems, but I have a guy looking for a job for me as a reading specialist. That's a job I could do and I think I'd like it."

"Budget problems make it tough all over. When I applied

with the sheriff's department, there were 2000 applicants for only about 20 positions. I applied more as a lark than as a serious candidate, but I got lucky, I guess. Maybe my work at the University helped a bit. Besides taking courses in law enforcement, I was part of security on campus before I graduated."

"Does the sheriff here care about gender, race quotas or anything like that?"

"I don't think so, Candi. All of Sheriff Dempsey's staff is working to get the most qualified personnel possible. My educational background helped me a lot. I'll bet with your college education and military background, they'd snap you right up."

Pointing over to where Pam had hung her service belt, Candi said, "I don't know if I'd like a job where I have to carry a gun, Pam."

"I didn't either when I applied. But they taught me that law enforcement is very important and sometimes police officers need a little help. Your Marine Corps provides a good weapon for Uncle Sam to use in keeping the peace."

"Pam, I think I'll do like you did before you applied. I'll go to your headquarters tomorrow and at least apply."

Pam went over and hugged Candi. "I'm glad. It would really be nice if we worked together. Now that you're getting applications at two jobs, does that help you to decide about the Marine Corps?"

"Not quite yet. But if I get out of the Corps, I'll need a job. Applying for jobs doesn't mean I'll get one."

"Be prepared to work hard tomorrow. An application to work as a deputy requires you to fill out a very long application form. You not only need to give them your background, but they want to know about your family and your education, military experience, driving records and a lot of other stuff. Candi, above all, tell the truth on each question. Any little untruth will disqualify you."

"Don't worry about that, Pam. They also ask information about that stuff in order to become a teacher. The Marines require some of the same information."

The next morning, following Pam's directions, Candi went out to the main headquarters of the Pima County Sheriff.

Before entering the front door, she noticed a small monument honoring several men and women who had been killed in the line of duty. The monument evoked a tear to come to her eyes since the names followed these words, "Lest we forget." She thought of Jim, and silently said, *I'll never forget you, darling.*

At the desk, she was given the application forms consisting of many pages, and then was seated in a room to fill it out along with several other candidates.

When she arrived back at the apartment, Pam met her at the door wearing a big smile. "Well, did you fill out the application?"

"I did," Candi responded while returning the smile. "A lot of people were filling it out besides me."

"Did they give you any idea when they would notify you about taking some of your tests?"

"As I handed the application to the receptionist, she said that it would take several weeks, and then they'd call me." Shifting gears, she added, "I hope that you planned for us to eat out tonight because I'm bushed."

"Two pieces of news first. The landlady told me that the apartment next door is available now if you want it. We could be neighbors instead of roommates. I'd like to keep you around, so let's go look at it. She gave me the key. And, the school district called. They could use a part-time reading specialist. It seems that one of theirs got herself pregnant and wants the rest of the semester off."

After looking at the apartment, Candi said, "Pam, I'm going to Oceanside the day after tomorrow if I get the reading job. Can you get off to go with me? It's a long drive if I have to go alone. I think I'll resign my commission, so I'll call Colonel Kincaide after the interview if I'm offered the teaching job. And, if that happens, I'll take this apartment. Now, let's lock up and go get some Mexican food. After filling out that application at the sheriff's office, I think I deserve a couple of enchiladas."

"I think we both do, Candi. I'm glad that we're going to be neighbors. I'll trade days with Amanda and go to Oceanside with you."

"I'll only be a minute. I've got to get out of this dress and into something more casual. I'm a messy eater when I'm chowing down at a Mexican restaurant." Chuckling she added, "The trip to California is on only if I get the job at the school, and Colonel Kincaide signs my release. I'll have to stay in the reserves, though, but that's okay with me because I don't want to completely lose touch with the Corps. If something big comes along, I want to be a part of it."

CHAPTER 6

———•———

"WELL, MISS ADAMS, YOUR PAPERS all seem to be in order, and I think that you will do a good job for us. Can you start on Monday?" Ivan Judd, the principal of Ocotillo High School, smiled across his desk, hoping that Candi would answer in the affirmative. He was not only impressed by her transcripts and application papers, but by her bearing and appearance.

"Yes, Sir. I have to go to Oceanside, California, and get my release from the Marine Corps; but I really don't have to go if you need me to start now. My commanding officer, Colonel Kincaide, said he'd mail my papers. However, I do want to say goodbye to some friends of mine who are Marines stationed there."

"That's okay with me, Miss Adams. I'm assigning you to two English teachers who have way too many students in their classes to handle alone. You'll work with Mrs. Hendricks in the morning and Mr. Evans in the afternoon. Come with me now and I'll introduce you to them. They're both excellent teachers, but they need some help because of overcrowded classrooms."

While walking down the hall, Mr. Judd nodded to several students and teachers as they darted back and forth. They walked out the door that led to the outside. Candi saw that there were four classrooms in each pod, and the ones in back had entrances from the sidewalks leading into the classroom. Judd knocked lightly on the door of a room numbered 203. Almost immediately, the door was opened by a short, elderly woman.

"Miss Adams, I'd like you to meet Mrs. Hendricks. Helen, I'd like to introduce Candi Adams. She'll be helping you starting next week. She's a certified reading specialist, and I think she can help you."

"How do you do, Miss Adams," smiled the older woman. I sure will welcome your help. I've got 44 students in one of my classes." As they shook hands, Candi was reminded of Miss Shreve, one of her favorite high school teachers. They both were probably nice women who could ask students to excel.

"I hope that I can help you, Mrs. Hendricks. I've never taught school before, but I'm sure that with your help, I can learn the ropes."

"I think she'll do fine, Mr. Judd. Well, I better get back to my students. I'll see you again next week, Miss Adams."

Candi said, "I'm looking forward to working with you."

"Now we'll visit Mr. Evan's class. It's just across this sidewalk in room 104." Judd led Candi the short distance across the sidewalk and knocked on a door that led into another classroom. The door was opened by a tall, good-looking man.

"Candi Adams, I'd like you to meet Joe Evans," the principal said. "Joe, this is Miss Adams. She'll be helping you starting next week with your crowded Junior English classes."

There was considerable noise from students while Joe and Candi shook hands.

"Excuse the noise, Miss Adams. We're trying to cast our reading of *Macbeth*. A lot of the boys want to play Macbeth especially if there's sword fighting."

Joe Evans appeared to be about 25. He was dressed in a very casual manner. He wore a long-sleeved, yellow shirt without a tie. Candi felt that she liked him almost immediately because of his winning smile.

"I hope that you'll still be doing *Macbeth* when I come aboard attempting to help you. It was my favorite of the four or five Shakespeare plays that I read in high school."

After leaving the classroom and returning to the principal's office, Candi was invited to have a cup of coffee with Mr. Judd. When his secretary brought the coffee in small plastic cups, Mr. Judd said, "Candi, you need to know something about Joe before you start working with him."

As Judd hesitated while forming his thoughts, Candi became a little nervous about what he wanted to say.

"A few months ago, Joe's wife was killed. She was coming

home from work when she was hit by a drunk driver. They were a very happy couple with a cute little girl. The accident almost broke Joe's heart, and it's still like pulling teeth to get him to laugh and be his old self. About the only place that he seems to be his old self is in the classroom. The board and I wanted him to take a long leave to get over it somewhat, but he insisted that he wanted to work after a short period of mourning."

"Mr. Judd," Candi said, "I believe I know how he feels. I recently lost someone near and dear to me. I'm trying to get back to normal after my fiancé was killed in a helicopter crash."

"I'm sorry, Candi, I didn't know that. If you need more time, I'll give it to you."

"No, Mr. Judd. I'm a little like Mr. Evans. I have to have something to take my mind off my loss. We'll probably both get along because of the recent loss of a loved one."

When Candi came back to the apartment, Pam was beaming. "Let's go to California, Candi. I've got three days off. I knew that you would get the job at school. I can tell by your face that you're happy about it."

"Let's leave in the morning. Meanwhile, I need to rent the apartment next door. And then let's go out for dinner—on me."

"Okay, as long as it's Italian. I know of a great place on Broadway."

Candi noticed that Pam carried her pistol in her purse

when she was dressed in civilian clothes. Candi wondered about that but didn't want to ask.

They arrived at the restaurant a few minutes before the rush hour. Both ordered a glass of red wine and were just taking the first sips when Candi said, "Pam, there's the man I'll be teaching with. His name is Joe Evans. I believe he's with his little girl. Can I invite them to eat with us?"

"Sure. The little girl with him sure is cute."

Candi got up and went up front and invited Evans and his little girl to sit with them.

"Okay, if you don't mind," Joe said. He looked down at his little girl and whispered, "I hope you remember your manners around these nice ladies."

After all the introductions were made, Joe and his daughter, Margaret, were seated.

Before they could look at the menus, Margaret spoke. "I sure like your name, Candi. I'll bet you're sweet, aren't you?" Margaret chuckled at her own joke, and the others laughed as well.

Candi smiled broadly, "Not always, Honey, but I try to be."

Then Margaret turned to Pam, "You said that you're a deputy. Is that a policeman?"

Pam laughed, "I'm a sort of a *policewoman*. I work for the sheriff."

Joe said, "Peggy, let's eat before you ask so many questions."

"Okay, Daddy, but can I ask Pam if she has a gun? I thought all police carry a gun."

"Sometimes when I'm on duty and in uniform, I wear a gun, but I hope that I'll never have to use it."

In spite of her father's admonitions, Margaret kept up a steady stream of questions. Both Candi and Pam enjoyed her almost-constant stream of chatter. Joe said little as they ate.

"How old are you, Peggy?" asked Candi. "Can I call you Peggy?

"Sure. My daddy calls me that, except when he's angry. Then he calls me Margaret Evans. My kindergarten teacher always calls me Margaret, though I don't think she's angry."

Peggy showed them the fingers of one hand as she said, "I'm five and a half. Next year, I'll be going to school, but I already know how to read."

"That's wonderful, Sweetie. What is your favorite story?" Pam asked.

"I like *The Three Little Pigs* best. I can read it, but I like it best when Daddy reads it. He makes sounds like a wolf and squeals like a pig. He tells me stories that aren't in books, too. I like them better than those in the books because he talks like wolves and things."

Candi said, "I'll bet your daddy's a great storyteller, isn't he, Honey."

As they all got up to leave, Candi asked, "Peggy, I haven't had a good tight hug in a long time. Do you suppose that you could give me one?"

Margaret smiled and got up on the seat of the booth. She threw her arms around Candi and squeezed as hard as she could.

"Me, too, Sweetheart. I need a hug if you have another one."

Peggy again stood on the seat and hugged Pam who pretended that the hug was too tight.

When they were all outside, Joe shook hands with the women, and that was followed by Peggy shaking their hands as well.

As they were about to go to the parking lot, Candi said, "Joe, if you ever need a sitter for your beautiful daughter, I know where you can find two of them. She's really wonderful."

"Thanks, both of you. I think that she needs lots of love now, and you folks gave her some tonight."

After they said their goodbyes, Pam said, "That little girl is so wonderful that I hope you weren't just saying that we'd babysit with her. I want to do it very much."

Candi said, "I wanted a little girl of my own just like her after Jim and I were married."

Pam said, "Let's get home and to bed so we can leave for San Diego early in the morning and get to the beach.

After they arrived in San Diego, Pam and Candi checked in at a motel very close to the beach.

"Let's hurry and get down to the water," Pam said excitedly. "I'm too much of a desert rat not to want to see the ocean occasionally. We can also probably get a great fish dinner there."

Candi smiled, "Okay, but I have to do a little ironing before we get to Camp Pendleton."

When they got to the beach, they spent time admiring the ships in the harbor and watching the tide. As dusk came, Pam said, "Okay, enough of this walking around. Let's find a good restaurant. I'm starved, and I think it's my turn to pay the bill."

After a short walk, Pam spotted a nice restaurant. "Let's eat there, Candi."

"Please, Pam. Not there. Let's find another one." Pam was pointing to the one where Jim and she had their glorious meal when he returned from the Mid East. *If we go in there, I'll spend all my time crying. That's where I fell in love with him.*

Pam saw the stricken look on her friend's face, and without further ado, said, "I think I see a good one across the street."

They had a delicious meal, and then walked along the coastline for awhile before they returned to the motel. Candi ironed her uniform while Pam talked about some of the things they could do after Candi's visit to the Marine base.

After showering and dressing the next morning, Pam whistled, "Wow, Candi. That uniform makes you even more beautiful."

When they got to Oceanside and the base, Pam became amazed at the size of Camp Pendleton. She gawked out of the window as she saw Marines doing close-order drill in the various areas.

As they entered Colonel Kincaide's office, the sergeant at the outer office desk beamed as he recognized Lt. Adams. "I'll tell the Colonel that you're here, Ma'am. He's expecting you."

When they were admitted to his office, Kincaide graciously asked them to sit after Candi introduced Pam.

"I'm sorry that you want to return to reserve status, Lt. Adams, but I have your papers right here. By the way, I wrote a glowing letter of recommendation to the sheriff's office in Pima County, Arizona. I think that whatever you do, you'll do it well."

He went to his file cabinet and took out a package and handed it to Candi. He said, "This is for you. Mitchell's mother sent it to me to give to you. This is the flag that was draped over his coffin at Arlington. The note that came with it said I was to give it to you."

Again, after concluding their business, Kincaide came around the desk to shake the hands of both women. But Candi teared up and folded into his arms saying, "No wonder the Corps is so good with men like you running it. I'm sorry I did that Colonel, but I'm going to miss you and the Corps so much." The Colonel drew her close and saw tears spilling out onto her cheeks.

When they left the Colonel's office, they went to the O

Club. "There are some people, I have to say goodbye to. They said that they'd meet me there."

Several of her friends were there. Each one took turns hugging and kissing her. All wished her well and promised to come to Tucson to visit with her. As they were leaving, Tim Monahan came around from behind the bar saying, "Just a minute, Lieutenant. You can't leave without this. He hugged and kissed her regardless of any Marine Corps rules prohibiting it. After leaving the base, Candi stopped at a service station to fill the gas tank and change into civilian clothes.

Those Marines really like you, Candi. I thought that sergeant was going to hold you so tight that you couldn't breathe."

Candi laughed, "Don't remind me of that Pam. I had a difficult time making the decision to leave. But this visit brought back some memories that I want to get rid of."

"I wish we could stay longer. That bartender was really good looking."

Candi opened the package and smothered her face with the flag.

They drove up the coast to Disneyland and enjoyed the excitement that place always offered. After that, they went to Santa Monica and again walked up and down the beach. They checked into a motel there and went out and had a delicious meal in Beverly Hills at a restaurant called <u>A Little</u>

Bit of Sweden. It was the first time that either woman had a true smorgasbord meal.

The next morning, they drove back to Tucson. Again, they shared the driving.

When they got to the apartment building, Candi went to Pam's place where they sat down and talked about the wonderful time they had on the coast.

The next morning—the last day that Pam had off—they went furniture shopping for Candi's apartment. When the stores delivered the furniture, Candi worked hard getting the furniture in the right place. The apartment manager's son hooked up her computer, TV and microwave oven. After all this was done, Candi thought, *Well, I guess I'm in my first home. I hope that whatever happens now will reduce my sorrow and bring me some happiness.*

CHAPTER 7

———————

THE DAYS, EVEN THE WEEKS, seemed to fly by for Candi. The first thing she did when she came home from school was to look through her mail to see if the sheriff's office had sent a notice. There was nothing for several weeks and Candi began to believe the department had either lost her application or she was was rejected without even an interview. But happily, when she came into her empty apartment, she had school work to do which kept her from sitting down and staring into space thinking of Jim and crying.

She was becoming more comfortable with the students, and she found Helen Hendricks and Joe Evans extremely helpful and forgiving of her mistakes. After a few days of just sitting in their classrooms watching Helen and Joe work, each gave her a small group of students to take into a vacant classroom or the library to try improving their reading skills as well as trying to keep them up with the lessons in the larger classroom.

The first time she had her "own class," she asked each

student why they had difficulty keeping up with the reading required. She got various answers to this such as "It's boring," "It's too hard," "I never liked literature," etc. After being with them for a few minutes, she knew that her first step was to try to get them to see the joy of reading. She talked about some of the books that started a spark in her that caused her to find joy in reading.

Each day she went over nearly the same lessons that the full-time English teachers were doing, but she tried to "liven it up" a bit with drama, humor and questions that led them often to a new perspective. For example, when Macbeth left the dinner party in honor of the visiting king and gave his wife reasons why he wouldn't and couldn't kill King Duncan, Candi talked about his reasons and explained that he had the honor of a great soldier. She selected a boy in the class to play the part and then selected a girl to be Lady Macbeth. As the girl read the reasons why he should murder the King, Candi forced her to be like the spider who urges the fly to come into her nest. The kids laughed when she came to the final argument: "If you love me, you will do it." They talked about situations where they had used that argument or heard it from someone else. Nearly every one of them had a story that proved that Shakespeare knew what he was talking about.

Without reading the whole play in cast, Candi talked about the story until she came to a speech that she felt would cause some discussion. She had each of them audition for the part of Malcolm when he was informed that his father had been murdered. Each had to say the three words that the actor used, "Oh, by whom?" As each student did it a little differently, the laughter could be heard all the way to the principal's office.

Every day, she saw that most of them were enjoying the experience and their attendance improved. One day, she said that the homework for the girls was only to memorize the witch's recipe for calling up the evil spirits while Macbeth watched. She was pleasantly surprised that all the girls had done it and loved doing it. Again laughter filled the room.

"Just wait until you get to do Lady Macbeth's hand-washing speech. I'll bet you'll really do a good job with that." She promised the boys that they could have Macbeth's speech after he is told that his wife is dead.

Again she was surprised that all the students had read ahead on their own to get to those speeches. She discovered that making the lessons fun and letting them participate was beginning to light a spark in some. When they went into Joe Evans' classroom to take the test on *Macbeth*, none scored less than a C, where before most had gotten Ds and Fs. That pleased Candi and Joe, but what pleased her more was Joe telling her that she had done a great job with them.

The next day in their little class she told each one how wonderful they made her feel by the success they had on the test. One of the boys spoke up, saying, "Miss Adams, you make reading fun."

Another thing that made time slip by was little Peggy.

After the first time that Joe had asked her to sit with his daughter, both Pam and Candi started asking Joe if they *could* do things with the little girl. They took her to movies, bookstores and ice cream parlors, and had more fun than the little girl did.

She and Joe took to drinking coffee together, both in the faculty room and often after school at a nearby coffee shop. She was surprised when he told her that he had spent two years in the Marine Corps Reserves. They exchanged stories about that, and both talked to the other about their lost loves but only after quite a number of coffee sessions.

One day before school started, Joe came to her and asked, "Candi, would you be comfortable taking my classes on Friday. I told Mr. Judd that I thought you could handle them as well as your group and better than a substitute could. Ivan said that he'd allow that if you were willing."

"Of course, I will, Joe. I assume you need to be absent on Friday?"

"Yes, I will be. I need to fly to LA because my mother wants me there. She's going in for a small surgery. Could you stand having Peggy for three days?" He added the last question with a smile because he knew that both Candi and Pam would love to have her for the whole weekend.

"That would be our treat, Joe. I'm sure that Peggy would enjoy the "sleep-over" with me. I'll drop by tonight to pick her up and the clothes that she'll need for the weekend. Are you planning to come back Sunday evening?"

"Yes, my sister is flying in from Cincinnati on Sunday to stay with Mom. My flight back to Tucson will get me home about 9:00 pm. I really hate to put all this on you because you might have other plans. If you do, her grandmother Martha will take her."

"Please don't be sorry, Joe. We were going to ask you to let Peggy stay with us for a weekend anyway."

When Pam heard that they had Peggy for the weekend, she was over-joyed.

On Friday night, after having a meal at MacDonald's (Peggy's choice), Candi and the little one watched TV for awhile and then she read her a bedtime story after her bath. As Candi was telling the story of *Snow White*, Peggy crawled up on her lap and fell asleep. Before she carried the little girl to bed, Candi just sat there cuddling her. She dreamed about what might have been with Jim if they had been able to marry and have a little one like Peggy. She found herself crying for the first time in weeks. She didn't stir until Pam came in and saw her friend holding tightly to the sleeping girl and crying.

Through the rest of the weekend, both women enjoyed taking Peggy to many places. Peggy said, "I like you calling me Peggy. I like that better than Margaret and that's what Mom called me." When they went out, she always tried to be in the middle holding hands with both women.

On Sunday night after her bath, Peggy again went to sleep in Candi's arms. She carried the little girl to bed and then turned on the TV without paying the slightest bit of attention to it. After awhile, she turned the set off and opened a book she had been reading only to find that she was just daydreaming again and ignoring the story.

When the doorbell rang, she opened the door for Joe. "Peggy's asleep, Joe. Come on in." Joe came in and sat down in the offered chair. "How about a drink, Joe?"

"If you have an extra beer, I'd appreciate it, Candi. I hope that Peggy wasn't too much for you and Pam."

"Joe, how could that be? We both love Peggy. We'll sure miss her after you take her home."

They sat quietly talking while drinking the beer. Joe drank his slowly while he explained about his mother's small operation. When they went into the bedroom to get Peggy and her clothes, both stood by the side of the bed just watching the little girl sleep. Almost without thinking about it, Joe put his arm around Candi as they stood there. Then he pulled her close and kissed her—at first tentatively and then a little more passionately. She came into his arms, kissed him in return, and then put her head against his chest while each had their arms around the other.

In a few seconds, she pulled away. "Joe, I think you should pick her up and I'll take her clothes to your car."

"Candi, I'm sorry about that. I just felt…I…"

"I know, Joe. I felt the same way. It's been a long…Let's get started."

When they got out to Joe's car and put Peggy down, he reached for her again. "Thank you, Candi."

She put her arms around his waist and reached up and kissed him fervently, and then she turned around and walked hurriedly away without another word or a backward glance.

CHAPTER 8

———

THE NEXT MORNING AT SCHOOL both Candi and Joe acted toward each other the same way they had all semester—mentor and student. During the lunch hour in the faculty room, Joe talked and laughed with the coaches, and Candi drank coffee with Mrs. Hendricks. But as the students were leaving at the end of the school day, Joe said, "Miss Adams, would you have a cup of coffee with me at Clarks? Mr. Judd asked if I'd talk to you."

Candi smiled, "Oh, oh, am I in trouble with the principal? I haven't been sent to the principal's office since the sixth grade because I pulled a boy's hair."

"Quite the opposite. See you there in 30 minutes?"

When Candi arrived at Clark's, Joe was already seated and drinking coffee. "Thanks for coming, Candi."

Jean, their regular waitress, came over and asked, "Same as usual, Candi?"

"Yes, please, Jean."

When Jean went to get her coffee, Joe put his hands over

hers. "Candi, I'm sorry for what happened last night. I hope I'm forgiven."

"No problem, Joe. It was just one of those things. What was it that Mr. Judd wanted with me?"

Joe smiled. "He spent my whole free period asking questions about you and how you got along with the kids. I told him that you were very good and had most of your students eating out of your hand."

"Thanks for the kind words, Joe."

"That's not all, Candi. After he asked me a dozen questions about your teaching, he left and went into Mrs. Hendricks's class. While her kids were reading, she gave you a glowing report as well. He said that he wants to see you before school in the morning. I think he's going to hire you full time next year."

Candi's face reddened, "Did he say that?"

"Yes, in the oblique manner that all principals seem to use. He's very impressed with you."

"But, Joe, I understand that the whole English department is returning and so is the reading specialist whom I am filling in for. Where would I fit—the budget being what it is? There are lay-offs throughout the system."

"Miss Weaver is going to get married this summer, and she and her husband are moving to Rhode Island. You would take her place in Freshman English and Remedial Reading I would think."

"But I've already got my application in at…"

Joe interrupted, "Candi, I hope you don't take a job there. Being a cop is dangerous, and I'd worry about you. I know that you trained with the Corps, but …"

She smiled, "Thanks for your concern, Joe. I don't think there's much chance of my getting a job there. I haven't heard from them since I applied. Pam says it takes a while for them to decide who will be given a shot, but it's been a long while now since I applied."

"Would you take the job if they accepted you?"

"Now I don't know, Joe. I love teaching very much and I like this school, but…I just don't know. Maybe Ivan won't offer me a contract, and then it's a dead issue."

When Pam went into her apartment that evening to join her friend in their daily Pepsi together, she asked, "Candi, what's the matter? You look far away this afternoon."

"Joe thinks that I'll get a contract for next year at school. It'd be a permanent position for at least one year. After that… who knows with budgets like they are."

"That's good, Candi. It must mean they like you there."

"But what if the sheriff's office calls me in?"

"You should've heard by this time. Give me your phone. I'm going to call a friend in personnel right now." It was so late in the day that Pam got no answer.

The next morning Candi arrived at school almost an hour early and waited in the office for the principal to arrive. After she waited only a few minutes, Judd came in like a whirlwind. When he noticed Candi, he said, "Please come in, Miss Adams. How are you today?"

"Fine, Mr. Judd. And you?"

Judd laughed, "If you had my job, you'd start every day with at least a small headache."

When they were both seated, Judd said, "I'll cut right to the chase, Miss Adams. I expected you to be a good teacher when I hired you, but you've far exceeded my expectations."

"Thank you, Sir. This is a great place to work, and the kids are wonderful."

"I've observed you in class, Miss Adams, and I've also talked to several members of the faculty. Mrs. Hendricks and Mr. Evans speak very highly of your talent and abilities. I've even talked with a few of your students. They also give you high marks. Will you consider taking a full-time job here? I think you'd be a wonderful addition to the faculty."

"Sir, I don't…"

"Joe told me about your application at the sheriff's office. You'd probably make a good deputy, but I KNOW that you're an excellent teacher, and I believe that you love teaching. Take a few days to consider your future, Miss Adams. Your signed contract isn't due for three weeks. And, Candi, I personally think your future is in teaching."

When the bell rang for the beginning of the school day, Candi bid Mr. Judd goodbye, "Thank you again, Sir. I'll think it over carefully." She was a bit dazed as she walked into her class with Mrs. Hendricks.

That evening after work Candi rushed home because she needed to change for dinner. She and Pam were going to the Golden Corral for ribs, and she knew that she needed to go there in old clothes because of the dripping ribs.

When Pam came in, also dressed in old Levis, Candi asked, "Guess what, Pam?"

"Don't give me three guesses. One will do. You've been offered a full-time job at school."

"I have, Pam. And I want to discuss it with you."

"Okay, but let's do it over ribs before the late dinner crowd arrives at the restaurant." Pam knew by her friend's face that Candi was facing much the same problem as she had on whether or not to leave the Corps. *Life gives us many crossroads. We have to make decisions that may change our lives. Poor Candi has a few issues now: The school job, maybe she also has to decide about her relationship with Joe, and then for good measure, she may be called in for an interview with the sheriff's office.*

CHAPTER 9

THE 30 DAYS WOUND DOWN to the time when she must decide if she wanted to have a permanent spot on the faculty or if she wanted to continue waiting for word about a possible position as a deputy sheriff. *I remember something I learned in grade school "A bird in the hand is worth two in the bush."* Every time she had a good class in Reading Development she was tempted to sign the contract and relieve her anxiety about her choices. On days when she had to be in the office for something, she tried to avoid contact with Ivan Judd because he might attempt to influence her to choose teaching. At coffee after school with Joe, she hoped that he wouldn't bring up the subject either. After dinner with Pam, she always steered the conversation away from anything to do with the deputy job. Yet each day she sorted through her mail eagerly hoping for some word from the sheriff's office even if it were news that she'd been rejected.

She also wondered about her relationship with Joe since she didn't want it to totally end regardless of her decision.

One evening over coffee, she asked, "Joe, how is little Peggy coping without her mother? It's probably tough on her in kindergarten when her friends talk about their mothers, and she doesn't have one."

"I know it is, but my mother-in-law helps, and so do you and Pam. I hope there's no life-long trauma, and I think there won't be because of people like you."

"Do you mind telling me how you met Rosemary? If it hurts too much, let's change the subject."

"I can think about her now without too much pain. She worked in the Dean's office at the University, and I met her when I went there one day. I had to clear something up—I forget now what it was. I started talking with her while I waited for the dean. I think it was her smile that got me. I don't know that I'd ever seen a girl with such a beautiful smile and such happy eyes. I started talking with her, and right off the bat, I knew she had a great sense of humor. She made me feel so good I wanted to stay and talk to her even when the dean came out and ushered me into his office. When I left the dean's office, she was just clearing her desk and getting ready to leave for the day. I don't know what it was that prodded me to ask her if I could walk her to her car. She smiled and said, 'Sure, I need a little help with these books anyway.' I was so excited that she'd allow me to go with her that I dropped some of her books. When we got to her car, she opened the door and took them out of my arms. 'Thank you, Joe' she said, as she started her car and drove away. I was left standing there wondering about her. It was a strange feeling—something I never had before."

Candi laughed, "I'll bet you looked a little funny picking up the books you dropped. She probably knew that she gave you butterfingers. I think you and I felt the same way on first meeting our sweethearts. I know that my first encounter with Jim left me feeling a bit strange. Like you, I was charmed by his smile."

Joe smiled and continued his story. "The next day I went into the dean's office and just sat there looking at her as she typed. I knew I needed some excuse for being there, so I pretended that I needed to see the dean again for something. She looked over a couple of times and smiled, but went right back to work. Then she got up and walked over to me, 'Did you want to see Dean Beale?'

'No. I just came in to see you and ask you to have dinner with me.'

She laughed and said, 'Thanks for asking Joe, but I have other plans for tonight. Some other time, perhaps.'

After that, I went across the street and sat on a bench watching the dean's front door. I felt just like a sophomore in high school with his first crush. I remember that I felt guilty spying on her. Before she came out, a big pick-up parked in front. A huge fellow got out and walked up the sidewalk and went into the dean's office. Only a moment later, Rosemary came out, and the big guy was carrying her books in one hand and holding her arm with the other. She and he drove off in his truck. The green-eyed monster—jealousy—left me trembling."

"What did you do then, Joe? I'll bet you felt that you lost her even before you had her."

"I went back to my dorm with my head down, but the next day I was having a burro at Chico's, a fast food place near the campus, when she came in. She sauntered over to my table and threw down a book. 'Save me a place, Joe. I'll be back. I need a cup of coffee.' In a moment she came back and sat down. 'I hope you don't mind my sitting here, Joe. The dean went to a meeting and I closed the office early.'

'Is your boyfriend going to pick you up again today?'

'What boyfriend?'

She looked very puzzled.

'The guy that picked you up in the red pickup yesterday.'

She almost fell off her chair laughing.

'That was my brother Paul. He said he needed me to pick out a sport coat for him. Did you think he was my boyfriend?'

'I got that idea. Is your real boyfriend as big as Paul?'

Again, she began laughing, 'My last boyfriend got married last week.'

'Then if you're not busy, will you go to the movies with me tonight?'

'What do you want to see?'

She reached across the table and put her hands over mine.

Her hands were so beautiful that they sent an electric current through me.

That movie started my taking her out. We got married six months later. Candi, she was very beautiful and so full of joy. During our first year of marriage, Peggy came along. When that drunk hit her, the only thing that kept me going was Peggy."

"Thanks for telling me about her, Joe. We both are in the same boat, I guess."

When Candi got home, she wondered what was keeping Pam. She was usually home before Candi. When she didn't come after an hour, Candi began pacing the floor and worrying. Just as the sun set, a strange car pulled into the driveway. When Candi looked out, she saw a uniformed deputy run around the car and open the door for Pam.

When she saw her friend being helped around the car, she ran out to meet them. "Oh! My God! What happened to you, Pam?"

Pam looked up seeing Candi rushing toward her until she stopped in shock. Pam had her arm in a sling, her face was a mass of cuts and bruises, and her uniform was almost in shreds. She limped slowly forward and tried to smile at Candi. "Let me come into your place and lie down, Candi. I think I'm going to need some of your nursing skills."

When the male deputy left and Pam was stretched out on the couch, Candi knelt down beside her and began to cry while she asked if she could get Pam anything.

"Please tell me what happened to you. Did you have a wreck?"

"I guess sort of, Candi. I answered a domestic disturbance call. When I got to the house, I looked in through the screen door and saw a woman on the floor, bleeding and crying. Then I turned a little stupid and went in without waiting for backup. I was trying to get her up when a big jerk came out of the bedroom behind me. 'GET THE HELL OUT OF HERE, YOU BITCH! THIS IS NONE OF YOUR DAMN BUSINESS!' he shouted. 'I'll take care of her myself. She belongs to me.'

After I saw all the blood she had lost, I turned to face him and said, 'You're under arrest.' Before I could say anything else, he charged me and knocked me over. He slugged me a few times and then took off. It's a good thing that backup arrived then because Hank tackled the bastard and put the cuffs on him."

"Let me get you something to drink, Pam."

"Okay, Candi, but make it a double."

Candi brought her a drink and knelt down to wipe her face. Through a fat lip, Pam said, "Candi, teaching school may be rough, but at least you don't get beat up. Maybe you should stay in teaching. At least you wouldn't get your beautiful face rearranged."

CHAPTER 10

———◆———

CANDI TOOK TWO DAYS OFF to stay with Pam as she started recovering from her injuries. During those days, Candi prepared all the meals or else went out and brought food home from Chinese buffets or places like Taco Bell. She helped Pam get dressed and undressed as well as seeing to her medications and bathing.

Nearly every day Pam had visitors from her friends at the sheriff's department. When her visitors weren't fellow employees, they were insurance representatives or someone from the County Attorney's office. While Pam was busy with her almost steady stream of visitors, Candi cleaned her apartment, watered the flowers, as well as serving the visitors coffee and cookies. On the third day after Pam had suffered the injuries, Candi went back to school after being assured by her friend that she was well enough to cope during the day by herself. When she returned home after her first day back at work, she saw a car in the driveway that she hadn't seen before. *I wonder who it is this time. Maybe it's an old boyfriend who heard or read about her getting hurt. After all, this story was on television and in the newspapers often enough.*

When she opened Pam's door, she saw Pam sitting up talking with a very nice-looking man. He was dressed in sharply pressed gray dress trousers, a green dress shirt with an unbuttoned collar held in place with a beautiful bolo tie. Both Pam and the stranger had just finished laughing at something.

"Candi, I want you to meet my boss, Sheriff Dempsey. Clarence, this is my friend from Prescott that I told you about. Her name is Candace Adams."

The sheriff got up quickly and while shaking Candi's hand said, "I'm very happy to meet you, Miss Adams. Pam has told me about how much help you've been to her. I really appreciate your caring for Pam as you have."

"Thank you, Sir. The only problem that I have taking care of Pam is that she's so blasted independent. Many times she'd rather do it herself than have anyone help her." All three of them chuckled about that.

"I know how independent she is. She's that way at work. By the way, I've seen your application to join us, Candi," Dempsey said as he resumed his seat in one of the reclining chairs in Pam's living room.

"Let me make a pot of coffee, Pam. Do you drink coffee, Sir?"

He laughed, "Have you ever heard of a cop who didn't? Yes, I'd love a cup if you don't mind."

When Candi went back into the kitchen, Pam and her distinguished visitor resumed talking with each other. Candi brought coffee and cookies into the living room in a few minutes. Pam asked Candi to sit down on the nearby couch. "Miss Adams," the sheriff began, "Your application for a position in our department crossed my desk yesterday. I was very impressed by your experience in the Marine Corps. Your commanding officer, a Colonel Kincaide, wrote one of the finest letters of recommendation that I've ever read. We are getting ready to start training sessions for the next class, and, without revealing any secrets, your name is on top of the pile of candidates. You should have received a letter from us indicating that. Have you?"

"No, Sir, I haven't. I've been looking for one. I just assumed that you probably weren't interested in me."

The sheriff chuckled, "I think you must realize that like most government offices, we're often snowed under by regulations and paper work. I apologize for the delay, but, Miss Adams, we are most anxious for you to start training with us. I bet with you and Pam in the department, we would really have a dynamic duo."

"Thank you, Sir. But I've been offered a permanent position at Ocotillo High, and I have pretty much decided to take it because I've discovered that I love teaching."

"Miss Henry told me that you do very well with your students. I'm not at all surprised that you love teaching and are probably a good teacher. It's very important that our schools have good people to teach the kids. I had some great teachers at Bisbee High, but, like a dummy, I often didn't pay much attention to what they said. I'm sorry now that I didn't."

"When I came to Tucson, Sir, Pam urged me to apply for a job as a deputy, and she told me how important your department is. I guess that in many ways we try to do the same things."

Pam looked on while this dialogue was going on. She then interrupted, "Candi, the guy who that beat me up and did it to his own wife needed to be put in a place where he won't do harm to others. That's the main mission of the police everywhere. I believe that we need safe streets if our citizens are to be happy and productive."

"Pam's exactly right. We have our share of failures just as you do while teaching, but we constantly try to help the people of our county to enjoy a better life."

"Before you and Pam explained how dedicated you folks are, I was totally committed to teaching. You say that a training class is beginning. If I pass the next steps in the process of joining your department, can I still think about returning to teaching if I want a career in that instead of law enforcement?"

"Sure, Candi. May I call you Candi for now?" When she nodded, he continued, "Law enforcement isn't always for everyone. But I would sure like you to try it. Besides, the pay is a whole lot better than you probably make teaching." At that the sheriff chuckled. Then he added, "I think teachers should earn a lot more than they do."

Candi laughed, "I'm not entirely motivated by money, but it always helps. I very much wish they would pay teachers what they're worth. Maybe our citizens will someday realize how important it is to have good teachers and pay them what's right and fair."

"Pam and Candi, I have to go now. I'm very happy to have met you, Candi. I'm sure that you'll hear from us in a day or two outlining some of the procedures of our training program." As he rose from the recliner, he added, "Pam, you get well real soon. We need you back at work."

The sheriff shook hands with both of the women. When he was gone, Candi said, "Your boss seems like a good man. Is he easy to work for?"

"He sure is. He knows the law inside and out, and he always supports his officers. I wish sheriffs everywhere were like him."

By some happy coincidence, when Candi checked her mail, she found an envelope from the Pima County Sheriff's Department among her letters and bills. When she ran over to tell Pam waving the letter, her face showed her friend that she received the expected letter. Pam smiled and said, "Enough of this cabin. Let's go out and celebrate. I think that I want a glass or two of wine with Mexican food, so you have to drive."

"Are you sure? You're still a little wobbly."

"You'll help me if I stumble. Please, Candi, I've got to get away; even for a little while."

"I'll sure help you, but I bet you don't really need much because you're almost ready to go back to work."

"I won't be ready until we sit and chow down on a big plate of Mexican food."

CHAPTER 11

WHEN CANDI AND PAM HAD finished their meal and were lingering over coffee, Candi looked closely at her friend. Pam was smiling, but pain made it difficult for the smile to be natural.

"How long are you going to be off, Pam?"

Pam chuckled, "The boss told me to not even consider coming back for the next two weeks. Then I have to have a complete physical before I can return to work. Then I'll have to work a desk for awhile."

"Good. We're going to do a lot of walking for the next two weeks. But please, Pam, don't do much walking until I can go with you. I don't want you falling down with nobody around to pick you up."

"Okay. I'll follow my nurse's advice."

"Is that a promise, Pam?" Candi asked this while reaching across the table and grabbing both of her friend's hands.

Pam laughed, "Okay, Mom. I'll listen to your orders. By the way, thanks for helping me. I don't know what I'd have done without you. Now let's discuss something else. How did you like my boss?"

"He seems like a nice guy."

"Are you going to enter the training program at the academy? I think he really wants you to. Before you came in this afternoon, he told me that you were on top of the next group to go into the training."

"I think I will. School will be out, and it will give me something to do."

Pam laughed, "Candi, don't think that the training will be easy. I think that they acquired some of their ideas from the Marine's boot camp. It's tough and a lot of the trainees fall by the wayside."

"Well, tough training works for the Marines. I guess that the Pima County Sheriff's department is probably better because of the tough training. You survived it, Pam. What do you think of my chances?"

"You'll do fine, Candi. I don't think that you could forget your Marine training this soon."

The next day before school Candi went into the office and asked to see Mr. Judd. He stood up when she entered and motioned her to a seat. "Miss Adams, have you made a decision?"

"Yes, Sir. I'm going to enter the training class of the sheriff's department. But because of you and Mr. Evans and Mrs. Hendricks, I have had a hard time deciding to do that. I've loved my time here."

"Choosing to follow a certain path is often hard. I hope you've considered your decision well. I know that you are a fine teacher, and I know that our county sheriff's department will undoubtedly be better because of you."

"Thank you, Sir. I hope that I can hold up to its rigorous training program."

Judd came around from behind his desk to shake her hand. "Candi, we will miss you. If you ever decide to continue teaching, please contact me. I have some influence with the school system here, and I think that it will be easy to find you a position should you decide to continue teaching."

"Thank you, Sir. It gives me a good feeling to know that I'd be welcomed back."

With only two days left in the semester, the classes were busy just studying for finals and turning in books. After the finals, Candi was pleased that her classes did very well. Not one of her students got lower than a C on the final tests. *I'm so proud of them, I could bust.*

On the final day of school while they were getting their final checks, Joe stopped her. "Candi, Peggy would like you to have dinner with us tonight. Will you and Pam be our guests at El Charro?"

"I'd love to, Joe, but Pam has another date. Is it okay with Peggy if it's just me?"

"She'll be a bit disappointed because she loves both of you, but your coming will make her happy. We'll pick you up at around 5:00. Is that okay?"

"That's fine with me, Joe. I usually eat dinner fairly early."

Joe drove into her driveway a little before the appointed time, but she was ready and went outside to meet them before they could get out of the car.

They found that the restaurant was a bit crowded even at this early hour, but Joe had called in advance for reservations, and they got a good table. Both Peggy and Candi held onto each other so tightly that neither wanted to let go after they arrived at the table. Peggy added a few kisses even though she had given plenty while they drove to the restaurant.

While they were eating, Peggy kept up a steady stream of conversation aimed mostly at Candi.

When they left the restaurant, Joe asked, "Candi, there's a Disney film playing at the Mall. Will you consider going there with us? I hear that it's good."

"I sure will. I love movies. The characters are about nine feet tall, and we don't have to strain to see their faces. But remember that I'm buying the refreshments."

Peggy, seated between them, held both of their hands when the scary scenes were on. After the movie, Peggy asked, "Dad, can I spend the night with Candi? Please."

Before Joe could answer, Candi said, "I think that's a wonderful idea. Please let her, Joe."

"Okay, but you have to be home by noon tomorrow because your grandmother wants to take you shopping for a new swimming suit."

When they got to Candi's apartment, Candi invited Joe in for a drink. While Peggy colored with the book and crayons she found on Candi's table, she and Joe had a drink and talked.

"It's no secret, Candi that I wish you weren't going into training with the sheriff's department. Often that's very dangerous work, and I don't want you hurt."

"Thanks, Joe. I'll be okay. They train their people well, and I'm glad that you will worry about me some, but Pam said that most times the work is kinda dull and routine."

After putting Peggy to bed, they continued to talk until it was approaching midnight. As they got up, Joe put his arms around her and kissed her. She hugged him and returned the kiss.

Joe whispered while they held tightly to each other, "Please don't get so far in training that you and I can't see each other occasionally."

"Don't worry, dear. I think that I want to see more of you outside the classroom. And remember that Pam and I both want to see Peggy a lot this summer."

Before Joe got into his car, he turned and whispered, "Candi, I'm getting very fond of you." Then he pulled her close.

"Joe, I'm getting real fond of you, too. See you when I bring our little darling home tomorrow." She returned his kiss and then walked away.

Chapter 12

———

Candi arrived at the Academy early. She was looking forward to this new adventure but was a bit nervous about it as well. Pam told her some of the things they did at the Academy to train their officers so they could cope with the many various situations they might be involved in when they became full-time officers. She was joined outside the administration building by others who had arrived early. Then at 8:00 am, the door was opened and they filed in. Candi took a seat next to an older woman, and soon they were joined by a woman who was about the same age as Candi. The older woman whispered as she stuck out her hand to Candi, "My name is Joan Parmenter." Candi took her hand and replied that her name was Candace Adams, but she preferred Candi. They both turned to the third woman and introduced themselves. "I'm Louise Barrow," she said as they all shook hands and wished each other luck.

Looking around, Louise said, "It looks like we're a minority. I count 15 men. Girls, I guess we're going to have to work hard to keep up with them." Candi looked around seeing men of various ages sitting nervously. "I think they're as nervous as we are," Candi murmured with a smile. All the potential recruits stopped talking as several uniformed deputies came in and sat down in chairs facing the new recruits. From among them, a very pretty woman came forward to the microphone.

"Good morning. I see that you are all here and anxious to get started on your training." She smiled and added, "I know that many of you are understandably nervous. We all are when we face the unknown. You're facing 12 weeks of intensive training. You'll learn much here, and you'll discover that these lessons will help you when you graduate. Now, I'd like to introduce our boss, Sheriff Dempsey."

The only speaker in "civilian" clothes came forward with a smile. "He will say a few words of welcome." The pretty Sergeant then turned to face the Sheriff as he approached the podium and lifted up the microphone. Polite applause came from both those at the speakers' section and from the new recruits.

"Thank you, Sergeant. My name is Clarence Dempsey. I've been sheriff here for a long time, and we have a wonderful department. We hope that you folks will continue our fine work. As you know, Pima County is very large, but our few officers try to make it safe for all our citizens. That is our most important mission." He paused and smiled, "Today you start an intensive program that will help you in this job. The next few weeks will be grueling, but we hope valuable to you. As I look around, I see several of you have been in the military. This will be an advantage for you, but those of you without military training will soon catch up. We have several groups at the training academy right now. These groups are in different stages of training, so these small groups can get more individual attention. I'll leave now, but I want to remind you to listen carefully to your instructors. Thank you for applying to join our force. Good luck to you all." After another round of applause, the sheriff turned the mike over to the sergeant and walked out of the building.

The pretty sergeant came back to the mike. "Now, let me introduce you to some of your instructors. As the sheriff said, if you listen carefully as they go over their part of the program, you will learn many things that good law enforcement officers need and use."

In turn, the other officers came to the mike and introduced themselves. They all explained to the new recruits what it was that they taught. Each one told a short, funny story in an attempt to put the new applicants at ease.

During the first two weeks of training, the recruits were subjected to many tests. When they finished one written test, they faced physical training or training to use various weapons ranging from hand guns to shotguns. Then they returned to physical training or more written tests. There were only precious few moments to relax and unwind.

Candi thought, *Pam wasn't kidding when she told me this*

would be tough. I don't think Boot Camp in the Corps was as intensive as this is. If we survive, we'll be well trained.

Each night when Candi dragged herself home, she was met by a grinning Pam. After Candi sat down on her couch, she was asleep in only seconds. Pam had to wake her for dinner. Even while eating, Candi occasionally dozed off.

Pam, who had been given another two weeks of sick leave, tried to help her friend as Candi had helped her during her own rehab. "You look all done in. I think you're totally exhausted. Maybe you should call in sick and sleep around the clock."

"Pam, I think they're trying to kill us out there, but I'm going to stick it out. When I was in the Marines, they also tried to kill me, but they failed." Candi smiled as she told Pam of each day's activities. My friends, Joannie and Louise, are as tired as I am, but they're sticking it out. A few of the men are gone from our group. I guess the grind was too much for them."

One day when she came home, Peggy was there to greet her. She picked up the little girl and twirled her around several times. "Peg is here because Joe had to go to Phoenix and her granny had to go to Bisbee because one of her relatives came down with something."

While Pam was preparing dinner, Candi agreed to read to Peggy. In a few minutes, Peggy came into the kitchen and reported that Candi had fallen asleep just when the big, bad wolf was about to blow the house of sticks down. "Candi is very tired, dear. She's working very hard, so let's not wake her until supper is ready. Can you help me get some of this on the table?"

Peggy smiled, and took over the job of placing silverware around the table. When everything was ready, Pam said, "Okay, honey. You can wake up Candi?"

The little girl went into the living room and crawled up on Candi's lap. She took the book from Candi's hand and whispered loudly, "Time to get up, Candi. Dinner's ready." While she said that, she shook her until Candi roused.

"Sorry I fell asleep, darling. Where's the book that we were reading?"

"Dinner is ready, Candi. I helped Pam get it ready. Now come on, Lazy Bones. Let's eat. My dad sometimes calls me Lazy Bones when I have trouble waking up."

When Joe came in later, Pam was reading a story to Peggy while Candi was fast asleep on the couch.

Joe smiled when he saw her asleep. He whispered, "Did Peggy wear her out?"

"No, Joe. The academy is wearing her out." Since she spoke in a normal voice, Candi woke up. "Hello, Joe," she said in a drowsy voice. "I'm glad to see you."

"I'm glad to see you too, Candi. Pam says that the academy is wearing you out—even worse than Peggy does."

She sat up and rubbed her eyes as Pam said, "I've got a fresh pot of coffee ready. Sit down, Joe. Peggy, will you help me in the kitchen?"

When they were alone, Joe came over and sat down next to Candi and kissed her. "I'll bet that you're learning a lot, Candi. I hope that it isn't too much for you." He smiled and added, "Don't you long for a nice restful classroom out there?"

She leaned into his shoulder and giggled, "I sure do. But all of us are counting the days till it's over." She held his hand, and spoke in a voice barely louder than a whisper, "I miss seeing you." She squeezed his hand and stood up. "I'll go in and see what the hold up is in the kitchen. Joe saw that she staggered a bit when she started toward the kitchen. Before she got there, however, Peggy burst through the door with several saucers and put them around the table. This was followed by Pam who came out with a coffee pot and mugs.

During the coffee and cookie time, Candi amused them with stories about her training. She made it seem funny when she described some of the instructor's impatience with them.

When Joe and Peggy were ready to leave, Candi walked outside with them. She put an arm around Joe's waist and held the little girl's hand. When they got to the car, she kissed them both and said, "I'm off to bed. Long day tomorrow."

Chapter 13

"REVEILLE! REVEILLE!" Pam shouted as she entered Candi's apartment after unlocking the front door and going into the sleeping woman's bedroom. "Get up, Candi. You don't want to be late for your first day of work as a new Pima County deputy sheriff, do you?"

"Mmm," Candi sounded as she opened her eyes. "Thanks for the wake-up call but Reveille is usually done with a bugle—not by a neighbor shouting into a person's ear."

"I'll put the coffee on while you're getting yourself together."

"Okay, Pam. It'll only take me a few minutes. I have my uniform ready. I'll take a quick shower, comb my hair and put on some make-up while you make coffee and start the bacon," Candi said as she threw off the blankets and crawled out of bed.

"Go light on the makeup. You're a cop now, not a beauty trying to become Miss America,"

Pam was drinking coffee and reading the paper when

Candi came into the kitchen and said, "You must have gotten up early today. You're all ready for work while your lazy slug of a neighbor is still in bed."

"Well, dear, I went to bed before 9:00 while you and Joe probably stayed up until midnight."

Candi replied, "Joe and the sleeping Peggy went home before midnight, but I was still wound up a bit, and I watched some TV after they left."

Pam smiled, "It was nice of Joe to take the afternoon off and bring Peggy to the graduation ceremony. They were both so excited that they couldn't sit still when the sheriff announced that you were the honor graduate. Peggy wanted to run up to the stage and hug you, and she told everyone around her that you were her best friend. It was all Joe and I could do to hold her in her seat. She was as proud of you as she would've been if you were her mother."

"I was happy that all three of the women were in the top five. We worked together most of the time at the academy. I was so happy when you took us all to dinner to celebrate last night. Peggy really made a great impression on Louise and Joannie."

"Little Peggy treated you like you were a queen. She couldn't get closer to you. I know that she loves you like she would love her mother."

Candi laughed, "She loves you, too. It was just that I was in the spotlight yesterday."

"Anyhow, what did you and Joe talk about after Peggy went to sleep?"

"We talked about his classes and my new job," Candi chuckled.

"Did you do a little smooching when I left?" Pam asked.

Candi laughed aloud, "A little. He's a very nice guy, and I think I'm falling for him—big time."

"I know you are. You two look like teenagers sometimes when you're together."

"I thought I was being so clever about it. Is it that obvious?"

"Remember, dear, that I'm a trained investigator. Cops look for signs like that. You had some training about that if you remember."

"I think that both of us are going a little slow about that. Jim Mitchell and Joe's wife still are a big part of both of our lives. For right now, I want to be able to concentrate on my new job. Let's finish breakfast and ride to work together. I'm always nervous when I start something new. You can calm me down and make sure that I haven't forgotten anything that I'm supposed to take with me. Were you nervous on your first day as a deputy?"

Pam smiled, "I sure was. And I didn't have a good neighbor to calm me down. You're lucky that I'm around and know the ropes!"

"Do you know who's going to monitor me?"

Turning a bit serious, Pam replied, "He's one of our best

officers. His name is Paul Tallman. He's a veteran who has many years experience, but watch out! He's pretty strict on recruits, especially women. He doesn't allow many rookie mistakes." Pam laughed then. "Some of the guys call him the 'bull shooter' because of a mistake he made when he was just starting his work without a monitor."

"Bull Shooter? Why do they call him that? Does he do a lot of wild storytelling?"

"No. He literally shot a bull on his first patrol."

"You're kidding! Did he really shoot a bull?" Candi laughed. "It's hard to believe that."

Both women laughed together as Pam began the story. "He was patrolling the back roads on the way to Ajo when he saw that a rancher's fence was down and a fence pole was broken. Paul radioed in that he was trying to get the fence up a bit because the herd was heading in that direction. While he was trying to fix it temporarily, he saw an angry bull charging him. He pulled out his service revolver and shot the bull. He testified that the bull would have escaped and probably killed him if he hadn't shot it. I guess the county had to pay for the bull, but I don't know. All I do know is that the story appeared in the newspaper, and he got a lot of teasing from his friends in the department. It was so long ago that most of us don't mention it anymore. Please, Candi, don't tell him that I told you about it. I don't think he likes to think about that incident. Sheriff Dempsey had to talk him into staying with the department."

"I won't," laughed Candi. "but can he ever be nice to rookies like me?"

"Yes, but he doesn't smile a lot these days. His wife just left him and filed for divorce. She wanted him to quit, but he wouldn't so she left him. She took up with a baseball player on one of the major league teams while the team was in Phoenix for spring training."

When they got to the motor pool, Pam gave Candi a hug for luck and pointed to the several cars lined up ready to take the new deputies on their first patrol. Candi saw Louise waiting to be called and went over to talk to her. "Well, Louise, we made it this far. Good luck today on your first patrol."

"Good luck to you too, Candi. Let's get Joan Parmenter and have a coke after our shift and talk it over. Okay?"

"That'll be fun, Lou. Are you nervous?"

"You can bet your life. I'm going out with Hank Williams. Do you know who you're with?"

"Pam Henry said that I was with Paul Tallman. She said that he was a good, experienced officer. I hope that we can get along."

Both Louise and Candi were called and went up to an officer who pointed out their respective monitors.

As Candi went to the car he pointed out, she saw a big man smiling while leaning on the front bumper. As she got closer, she screamed, "**Jim! Jim Mitchell!** Then she stopped and almost fell because she was looking at the man she loved and who supposedly died in a helicopter crash.

CHAPTER 14

———

UNABLE TO BREATHE AND WITH tears gushing down her cheeks, Candi stumbled and prevented herself from falling by grabbing a nearby fence post. With her heart racing, she was very near fainting while looking at the man whom she thought was Jim.

Louise rushed over to her while calling for Pam to come and help. Paul Tallman also ran over to where several deputies were gathering and surrounding his rookie partner.

"What's the matter, Candi Why are you crying?" Pam asked with concern.

Folding into her friend's arms, Candi said, "I saw Jim waiting..."

Paul Tallman spoke, "She was coming over to my car when she stumbled. She was staring at me kinda funny..."

Breathing a bit easier now, Candi looked at the tall deputy. "You reminded me so much of a man that I once was engaged to that I thought you were him."

Wiping away her friend's tears, Pam released her to stand

alone. "She had quite a shock, Paul," Pam smiled, "but I think she's over it now. She told me how much she loved the man that she thought she saw. That bit of shock is probably pretty natural. Are you okay now, Candi?"

"Yes, I'm okay now, and, Mr. Tallman, I'm so sorry that this happened. Please forgive me. I'm looking forward now to working with you. Deputy Henry told me that you're one of the best."

Tallman smiled and spoke in an amused tone, "Okay. All of you people get back to work! I'm anxious to see this rookie begin her new career as one of Pima County's finest."

After the crowd began to disperse, Deputy Tallman grabbed Candi's arm and walked her quickly to his patrol car. "I'd make you drive, Rookie, but I'll let you calm down for a few minutes. We both might be at risk until you do."

Candi smiled, "Thank you. That was very embarrassing to do that on my first day with so many people around."

When they were in the car, Candi asked, "Deputy Tallman, may I call you Paul?"

"Yes, but only when we're alone in the car. Otherwise, I'm Deputy Tallman when anyone is around. The sheriff wants us to have a mentor-student relationship for a few days, at least."

For the first time since she left Pam's car, Candi smiled weakly. "Deputy Tallman, you look so much like a man whom I loved that you and he could almost be twins. When I saw you leaning against the fender, everything about you reminded me of him—the way you were standing, your expression, everything."

Paul chuckled as he started the engine, "Pam told me that your guy was a Marine. It's tough to lose someone you love. I know about that from personal experience."

As they drove to their patrol area, Candi looked him over closely and found that he was probably a little older than Jim, and the resemblance was really only superficial.

"Deputy Henry said that you were a very experienced officer and that I could learn a lot from you. Again I hope you can forget my momentary bit of weakness. I'm very anxious to do my best to be a good officer like you."

"It's forgotten now, Rookie. In the next couple of weeks, I'm going to see how much you learned at the academy. I guess your Marine training helped you there a lot. I heard that you are the honor grad in your class, so I'll expect you to be good. Remember that I'm depending on you to cover my butt when I need it, and I'll cover yours. That's lesson number one."

After driving for a few minutes, Paul pulled over and stopped. "Okay, Rookie. Let's see you drive awhile. You should do all the work, not me. Our main job in this area is looking for illegal immigrants and drug smugglers. Both always try to hide when they see our car, so always be alert. If we spot any border jumpers, we take them to Immigration and let them take over. They'll return them to Mexico. Keep your eyes on the bushes near the road and any ditches nearby."

Paul continued, "I don't know how much Henry told you

about me, so I'm going to give you my version of the story about the bull. Did Henry tell you that I shot one once?"

"She mentioned it briefly. It was on your first patrol alone, wasn't it?"

"Yeah, it was. One of our duties is to make sure the ranchers' cattle and horses don't get loose. We certainly don't want any livestock wandering onto a highway or going across the line into Mexico. I was trying to fix a fence for one of these ranchers when a bull charged me. I shot the son-of-a-bitch before he gored me. Sorry about the language, Rookie."

"Don't worry about that Deputy. Remember that I was in the Marine Corps. They sometimes use language that is a little rough."

After driving in silence for awhile, Candi noted something green in the bar ditch beside the road. She stopped to have a closer look. When the car stopped, a man in a green shirt got up and started running across the low desert country. Candi jumped out of the car and began chasing him. She was closely followed by Tallman. In less than a minute, the man stopped and raised his hands. Candi came up and pulled his hands together and fixed her soft handcuffs on both his wrists. The man began talking Spanish so fast that Candi couldn't even begin to translate much of it.

"He says that he needs water, Rookie, and his family is close by. Please go get our canteen out of the trunk and bring it here. I'll watch him."

When Candi came back carrying a canvass bag full of

drinking water, she held it to the man's lips while he drank greedily.

"Nesecito agua. Ayuda mi familia. Estan cerca. Por favor eneventrenla. Mi llamo es Victor Uribe. Por favor ayuda mi familia. Yo frie en busca de agua. Por favor ayuda mi mama. Yo pienso que esta o murio. Mi esposa y mi niňa estan alli."

"He says that his family is back there somewhere. He came ahead searching for food and water. They haven't had any for two days. We'll lock this man in our car and search for his family."

"Gracias. Gracias. Dios les bendiga."

When they began searching, they separated, but Paul said that they were not to get out of shouting distance from each other. "Remember, Rookie, stay alert and be ready for anything."

In a few minutes, Candi reached a deep wash. She looked closely in both directions and was rewarded with the sight of a shred of white clothing across the ditch in the shade of a tree. "PAUL, COME QUICK! I'VE FOUND THEM!"

When her partner came into sight, she ran to a place that allowed her to drop to the bottom of the wash. She hurried to the shaded area and found an unconscious woman and a whimpering young girl who was not over five years old.

"Por favor ayuda, mi mamacita. Yo creo que mi madre esta muriendo. Mi nombre es Maria."

After checking the woman for life signs, she picked up the little girl and held her close. Paul arrived in a minute or so and began to treat the woman by wetting her face with the cool water and placing the canteen to her lips. For a few seconds, the water merely dribbled down her chin, but then she began to swallow some. In a few minutes, he took the canteen to the little girl who was resting in Candi's arms but still sobbing. He found her little lips, and amid some choking, the little girl began to swallow the drinking water.

When the woman started saying something, Paul spoke to her in Spanish . "Don't worry. We found your husband. He's alive." He then tried to take the little girl from Candi's arms, but the girl held fast to Candi and began to fuss. "Rookie, can you carry the youngster while I help the mother back to our car?"

Paul and the woman, who was leaning on him, led the way across the wash and started up the incline. He reached back and helped Candi climb as she was busy carrying the youngster. When they got back to the car, the husband and wife came together mumbling words of gratitude to the two deputies. Candi put the girl into her mother's arms and passed the water bag around as the Mexican family drank the canvas bag almost dry.

"Gracias! Gracias! Dios les bendiga. Yo pago un hombre mil dolares Americano a llevar nos a la casa de mi hermano en Tucson pero el hombre no regreso. Mil gracias. Usted ha sido muy abable. Dios le bendiga"

"He says the Coyote who was to take them to Tucson didn't show up in spite of the fact that they paid him $1000."

He added, "This happens a lot, but they continue cheating people who give them their life savings."

"Put them in the back seat, Rookie, and turn on the air conditioning. We'll take them up the road to a restaurant I know and give them a sandwich before we turn them over to Immigration. I think they're about starved. I know the little girl needs a glass or two of milk." He continued, "I think they'll be all right after they rest and get something to eat. I'd like to get the son of a bitch that left them stranded."

About 20 minutes later, they arrived at a truck stop on the road to Ajo, and all of them went into a restaurant after Paul radioed their location and plan.

The sheriff's office notified Immigration and they were told to stay by the restaurant until they picked up the illegals.

When the bus came to pick up the family, the two deputies received handshakes and hugs of gratitude from the family. Candi was happy when she was rewarded with a smile from the little girl along with a very tight hug.

When the bus left, Paul turned to Candi, "Well, Rookie, you done good on your first patrol. We saved the lives of three people. Now let's go home. Remember, you drive." Paul almost smiled at her as they returned to headquarters so they could make a report.

"Now we do the damn paperwork, Rookie. We can't leave without doing that. I hope that your penmanship and computer skills are better than mine. If they are, we might even get through it before quitting time. Are your computer skills as good as I hope they are?"

CHAPTER 15

———⋅◆⋅———

WHEN THEY ENTERED HEADQUARTERS, PAUL led Candi to a large room with many desks. She saw several recruits at computers writing reports with an experienced deputy instructing them. Louise looked up and smiled, "How did it go, Candi? Our patrol was uneventful."

"We had a little action, Louise, but Paul was helpful because he knew what to do." As she spoke, Tallman motioned her to a seat.

"Come on, Recruit, we don't want to spend all day doing this. You get on the computer while I watch."

Candi took a seat at an unoccupied desk and began writing. Paul guided her over the necessary form. As she wrote, he nodded occasionally but didn't say much except to offer directions on how to fill out the form.

After she finished, Paul said, "Now sign it and put it in that basket over there."

When she got up, she noticed Pam waiting for her in the

next office. Pam came out and asked, "Well, Candi, how was your first day as a Pima County Deputy?"

Then looking over her shoulder to make sure Paul was no longer around, Pam added, "How did you get along with Paul? He's usually pretty tough on new recruits."

Candi laughed, "He didn't talk much, but he gave me a lot of terse lessons. How do you get along with him?"

"Let's get on the road and we'll talk."

On the way to the apartment complex, Pam smiled, "Tallman had a bitter divorce recently. He doesn't get along with women now as much as he does men. He gets very angry if a woman doesn't do things his way. I guess you got through the day okay because he didn't crawl down your throat while you were at the computer."

"He told me that he was divorced, but didn't go into detail. He did say that his wife didn't like his job."

Pam looked over to her, "Shirley told me once that she wanted a man who had very regular hours and didn't have to answer phone calls that took him away from home at all hours. They had some loud arguments about that, I understand."

"She wanted him to get another job? Is that it?"

"Not by a long shot! She started going around with a professional baseball player. When the jerk dropped her off one night after a dinner date, Paul beat up the player so bad that it was several weeks before he could play again. She filed for divorce after that and finally took up with her ball player on a more or less permanent basis. They moved to Seattle during the off season."

"How long ago was that?"

"Over a few months ago. Paul was suspended for a few weeks while the department looked into the fight with the ballplayer. Aside from that, Paul has an outstanding record with the department."

"Did you like his wife?"

"We didn't see much of her. She's a real sexy babe and flirted with most of the men that she came into contact with. She had very little to do with his friends from work—especially the women."

After Candi had hung up her belt and taken off her uniform, she fixed herself a glass of wine and sat down in front of the TV while she unwound. In a few minutes, Joe called wondering if Pam and she would go to dinner with him and Peggy. "I'll call you back, Joe. I'll go and ask Pam."

Before she could go to Pam's, her friend opened her door and asked, "Let's go out tonight. I don't feel like cooking."

"Your timing is pretty good. Joe just called and wants us to have dinner with him and Peggy. I told him that I'd ask you."

Pam smiled, "I'd love it. We haven't seen Peggy much since she started school. I'm dying to ask her how she likes it."

After agreeing to have dinner with them, Candi took off her sweats and took a shower. She put on a nice dress and fussed with her hair and makeup while she waited for Joe to come for them. *What's happening? This is the first time I've been concerned about hair and makeup since I went out with Jim.*

"Wow! That dress will knock Joe for a loop. Why don't you and Joe go to a nice romantic place and let me take Peg to McDonald's? She loves it there with all the things they have for kids."

"Pam, I want to play with Peggy too. But I'll ask Joe if that'll be okay with him."

Joe agreed to take her to a nice restaurant while Pam and Peggy went to McDonald's. "Peg likes their hamburgers and fries better than the expensive food in fancier places." Joe grinned while patting Peggy on the head saying, "Don't give Pam a hard time while you two have dinner."

Peggy asked, "Why don't you go with us, Candi? Don't you like hamburgers?"

Candi picked up the little girl and took her over to the couch. "I love hamburgers, Peggy. But Pam wants to take you to a bookstore after dinner. She wants to have you read to her, and your daddy and I have some things to discuss about school. We'll be back before you have to go to bed because I want you to read the new book to me."

After Pam and the excited little girl had taken off to their dinner date, Joe came over and kissed Candi. "You sure look beautiful in that dress. It brings out the color in your beautiful eyes. As the poet said, "She walks in beauty like the night.""

"Let's go," Candi smiled. "Maybe we'll have time for Lord Byron after dinner. Where do you want to eat?"

Joe chose a small Italian place. When they were seated and had made their menu suggestions, she and Joe tipped their wine glasses and smiled at each other. He smiled and asked, "And how's the new deputy that's going to bring law and order to Pima County? How did the first day go?"

She took his hand and replied, "It went fine, Joe. And how about school?" As she asked, she reached over and grasped his other hand.

After dinner and another glass of wine, they left the restaurant and got into Joe's car. Before starting the engine, Joe pulled her over next to him and kissed her passionately. She put her arms around him and returned his kisses.

"Candi, dear, please be careful on your new job. It scares me and I don't want you to get hurt."

"Thank you for worrying about me, Joe. I'll be alright though. And if I don't like it, I'll go back to teaching. However, the work so far is very interesting." She looked over to him and smiled, "And I have a boyfriend that I don't see every day at work."

He laughed, "Does this boyfriend have a little girl that she adores?"

She reached up and kissed his neck. "It's that little girl that makes him a good deal."

When they drove into the driveway, Peggy ran out shouting, "Look what Pam bought me, Candi. It's a whole book about Snow White—and I can read it. Come in and I'll read it to you and Daddy."

When they were seated on the couch, Peggy got on Candi's lap and began reading. "Pam helped me with some of the big words."

Both Joe and Candi were a bit surprised that Peggy did such a good job reading the book. She even read the bad queen's speech with a bit of drama imitating Pam's reading, and she laughed when she read Grumpy's words.

Pam went back to her own apartment leaving them a half pot of coffee. Soon after reading <u>Snow White</u> to them for the third time, Peggy fell asleep on Candi's lap. As Joe picked her up, he said, "She loves you and Pam so much, Candi. I don't believe that she could love a mother more than she loves you guys. I'm so glad that you came into our lives."

When they had gone, Candi sat on her bed thinking of what Joe had said. While she was getting her clothes off, she thought: *And I don't 'think that I could love her more if she was my own daughter. I guess I better get some sleep before I have to face Paul again on our patrol tomorrow.*

CHAPTER 16

———————

DURING THE NEXT SEVERAL WEEKS, Candi and Paul patrolled their assigned areas. During that time, Candi did all the driving and the giving out of tickets to speeders, writing the reports, and watching for vehicles that might be smuggling illegals or drugs into the country. They arrested several teenagers who were drinking alcoholic beverages while driving or who had illegal drugs in their cars. But during all their trips together, Paul offered only suggestions but never spoke harshly to her when he felt she had made a mistake.

Once after giving a speeding ticket to a teenager who was doing almost 100 miles per hour on a highway with a 50 mph speed limit, she turned to him before starting the car and asked, "Paul, you never say much about how I'm doing. Please tell me if I'm doing things right or wrong at least."

"You're doing fine, Recruit. I'd chew you out if you weren't." Both were glad that the air conditioner took hold and began to dissipate the late summer heat that had made the car as hot as an oven.

"Am I improving?"

"I'll tell you when you do things wrong, believe me."

One day, just before they were due back at headquarters, they saw smoke rising out of a residential neighborhood.

"Code 3, Candi. Let's have a look."

When they arrived at the scene of the smoke, they found the street crowded with people watching a house go up in flames while some men were spraying the flames ineffectively with a little garden hose. Candi jumped out of the car while Paul was on the radio calling for aid from a near-by fire house.

As Candi approached, she screamed, "THERE IS NO ONE IN THE HOUSE, IS THERE?"

Several people watching the flames shook their heads and pointed to an old woman who was standing near the house crying. As Candi was about to ask if she was the owner, she heard the woman moaning, "Please, somebody help me. Wimpy is still in there."

Candi asked the man standing next to the crying woman, "Who is Wimpy?"

"Her old dog," the man said. "It's too hot to…"

Before he finished speaking, Candi yelled to the man on the hose to spray her. The man didn't immediately respond, so Candi picked up the hose and pulled it out of his grasp and splashed water over herself and then ran into the house through an open front door.

Paul ran over from the car, "WHERE'S MY DEPUTY?"

"She went into the house, Sir. She's looking for Wimpy, Mrs. Garcia's dog," a man responded, while pointing to the crying woman.

"MY GOD! IS THERE ANOTHER WAY IN?"

Meanwhile, Candi crawled across the living room toward a barking sound coming from the bathroom. There she found a black lab lying under the sink. The dog had stopped barking and was motionless. Gasping for breath, Candi reached the dog's body and found the dog was breathing shallowly. Grabbing onto the dog's collar, Candi crawled back into the living room and found the front door now totally consumed by flames. She stood up and picked up the dog and ran through the flames and emerged from the house just as Paul was attempting to enter.

She was aware of some people cheering as she came out. Paul ran forward and grabbed the dog from her arms and put it on the ground and then turned to see Candi falling nearby. He ran over to her and found that she was gasping for air but was shaking her head indicating that she was alive in answer to his frantic questions.

The woman who had been crying came over and knelt down beside her. "Are you all right? Please say that you are." She was still crying as she knelt beside Candi on the ground.

Candi nodded in her direction and gave the woman a weak smile while whispering, "Is Wimpy alive?"

The woman smiled, "He's wagging his tail. I think that he will be okay, and I'm changing his name to Candi. God bless you, dear."

Candi saw a flashbulb go off while Paul grabbed her arm and lifted her off the ground. He continued to hold her arm as he dragged her to their parked car. The fire trucks had arrived, and the yard was being cleared of spectators while firefighters were dashing toward the house carrying big hoses alive with water that was being held on the flames.

"SIT THERE AND DON'T MOVE? I'LL REPORT TO THE FIRE CHIEF AND THEN WE'RE OUT OF HERE. DO YOU UNDERSTAND? FOR ONCE IN YOUR LIFE, LISTEN TO ME AND USE YOUR BRAIN!"

She didn't know whether he was screaming in anger or screaming to be heard over the noise of the spectators and firefighters.

Candi nodded weakly and sprawled down still gasping.

In a moment, a firefighter came over with a respirator and put a nozzle over her face. In a few moments, she was breathing normally and the man removed the nozzle. She sat up and heard Paul ask, "Is she going to be alright? Should I take her to a hospital?"

"I don't think it's necessary, Sir. I think that she'll be right as rain in a few minutes. She needs to get over the trauma though."

Candi closed her eyes and thought, *Thank God that I can breathe again! I don't know how I carried that heavy dog out.*

She was aware of Paul getting in and starting the car while she was still shaking with fear and anxiety.

When they were clear of the scene, she heard Paul screaming, **"YOU STUPID BITCH! WHY DID YOU DO THAT—AND FOR A GOD-DAMNED DOG?"**

"I don't know, Sir. I'm sorry. I know..."

"SORRY DOESN'T CUT IT! THAT WAS THE DUMBEST THING I'VE EVER SEEN! I DON'T KNOW IF YOU HAVE THE BRAINS OF A SMALL AMOEBA!"

When he looked over to her for any kind of response to his angry shouting, he saw her looking at him with tears flowing down her cheeks. He pulled over to the side of the road and parked.

"Stop crying, Deputy! I'm sorry that I screamed at you, but I was afraid I was going to lose you back there."

"Do you think that I'll be fired? I think I'm not..."

"The sheriff will want to speak to both of us about this," Paul responded.

As Candi was now shaking with loud sobbing, she managed, "Does the sheriff have to find out about my stupidity? Please don't tell him about..."

"Candi, I'm sorry I called you stupid. I just...please stop blubbering." After he spoke, he reached over grabbing her and pulling her over to him. He put his arms around her as she put her head on his shoulder.

"Candi, you are a wonderful person and you will make a great deputy." He held her with one hand and rubbed the other through her scorched hair. When her sobbing stopped, she looked up at him with questions in her eyes. Then he put a hand under her chin and kissed her.

"Can we not put my going into the fire in our report?" She asked in a low voice while looking into his eyes.

He smiled as he said, "Anything for a friend of mine. I'll think about how to write this up." She returned the smile as she slid back to the passenger seat.

When they got back to headquarters, he helped her straighten her uniform and he brushed away some of the black soot that was on it. As they entered the building, Paul said, "Go home now, Candi. I'll write the damn report. And please take a shower to get the soot out of your hair and off your face. Do you think that you should be examined by a doctor?"

"I don't need a doctor, but I do need a shower. Paul, please don't tell Pam Henry about my dumb trick. I hope she doesn't even find out that I pulled that stupid stunt."

CHAPTER 17

———

WITHOUT ANOTHER WORD, PAUL LEFT Candi on the sidewalk and strode up to the offices while she turned and walked into the parking lot and got into her car. She put her head down on the hot steering wheel and began to sob again. *He called me a bitch, no not even that—I'm a stupid bitch. He put his arms around me, I guess, because he knew that he'd hurt me, but I think he meant it about me being stupid. Should I quit before they fire me? They probably will when the sheriff reads his report. I know he's going to write about my stupidity. That's why I'm not writing the report and he is.*

Louise Barrow came by just then on her way to her car and noticed Candi just sitting with her head down. "Candi, is anything the matter?"

Candi looked up to see her friend. "I think I'm not cut out to be here, Louise. Deputy Tallman called me stupid. I think he's right and they'll fire me."

Louise ran around to the passenger side of Candi's car and

got in. "What happened today? Why did he call you stupid? That's one thing that you're not and you've proved it."

"I went into a house to rescue a dog. The house was on fire."

Louise scooted over and grabbed her friend by the shoulder and looked into her eyes still sparkling with tears. "You did a good thing! That's not stupid. Did you get hurt?" After looking closely at Candi's face, Louise noticed that her hair was scorched and her uniform was covered with ashes and burned spots. She also noted that a strong odor was clinging to her.

"Do you think that you can drive home? If so, I'll follow you to make sure you get there safely."

"I do need someone to talk to. My apartment isn't far from yours. I'd appreciate it if you'd come for a few minutes, at least. Right now I need a good friend's shoulder to cry on."

"Stop crying and wipe your face. I'll be right behind you. Please be extra careful while driving home. When we get there, I want you to tell me all about it."

When Candi drove up to her driveway, Louise was right behind her.

"Before we talk you should go in and take a shower. While you're doing that, I'll throw your uniform into the washer." Both women walked into Candi's bedroom where Louise helped Candi strip off her uniform and underwear. Candi smiled, "Thanks for being here Louise. I need a friend, and Pam went to Phoenix this afternoon."

Louise waited until the shower started and then picked up the discarded clothes, emptied the pockets and took all the dirty clothes out of the basket and went into the kitchen to throw the whole bundle into the washing machine. *She's usually so cheerful. Deputy Tallman must have hurt her terribly. I'd hate to think that she'll be fired. I guess that he can be a mean bastard. I've heard that from other people. I'm glad he's not my monitor. She deserves a second chance, but I don't know if she really wants one.*

While Louise was putting on a pot of coffee, Candi came into the kitchen dressed only in underclothes and a robe. She was trying to comb the tangles out of her wet hair.

"Sit down here. I'll comb your hair for you and try to get some of the scorched places off. Where do you keep your scissors?"

Candi looked up and smiled, "They're in the basket on top of my dresser, but you don't need to do this. I'll take care of it."

In a moment Louise was back with the scissors and began snipping at Candi's hair. "You smell a lot better Candi. All your clothes are being washed, and you look a lot better too."

"Thanks Louise. A shower and shampoo helps a bit."

"Now that I'm finished scalping you, let's have a cup of coffee or something stronger while you tell me all about the fire and the dog."

After relating the story to her friend, Candi felt a little

better. "I just wonder what Paul will tell the sheriff. He insisted on writing the report himself, but maybe he'll be kind and give me another chance. I wish Pam were here. I think she could find out because she has friends in the main office."

"Let's not worry about it. I think we both need a drink. Come home with me and I'll get out of this rig and we'll go some place nice. Do you favor a place that serves good wine?"

Candi stood up and hugged Louise. "That may be exactly what I need tonight. It'll only take me a minute or two to get dressed."

As they were getting into Louise's car, Joe and Peggy drove up and stopped.

"Where are you girls going?" Joe asked.

Louise replied, "We're going to dinner and to have a drink. Do you want to join us? I think Peggy will do wonders for a distressed deputy."

For the first time in over three hours, Candi smiled broadly. "We're on our way to getting a drink." Peggy ran up to Candi and leaped up into her arms. "Guess what Candi? The teacher said that I was one of the best readers in class!"

As she was hugging and kissing the little girl, Candi whispered, "That's no surprise, darling. You're the smartest young lady that I know."

Looking back at Louise, Candi yelled, "We'll meet you at your place, Louise."

After picking up Louise after she had showered and

changed, all four of them rode in Joe's car down Speedway to a nice quiet Italian restaurant. Candi had told Joe about the fire and dog but didn't say anything about what Paul had said and done. When they were seated and ordered dinner and wine, Peggy asked "Do you know the story of <u>Jack and the Beanstalk</u>, Candi?" Can I read it to you?"

"I think that I remember it, but I know both Louise and I would love to hear you read it."

Peggy read to them while they waited to be served and then finished the story after they were through with dinner and drinking coffee.

When they got back to Louise's apartment, Candi walked with her to her front door. "Thanks for helping me tonight, Louise." She reached out and hugged and kissed her friend. "And thanks for the hair trim, too."

"I loved doing that," laughed Louise. "I guess I'm a frustrated hairdresser."

Joe drove to Candi's apartment where everyone got out and went into the house. Candi could barely walk because Peggy was holding onto her leg so tightly that she felt like she was being held by an anchor.

They all sat on the couch and talked until Peggy started falling asleep.

"I guess we'd better go, Candi. Peggy is getting tired."

"Do you want to lie down on my bed, darling and rest while your dad and I talk a bit? We won't be long?"

"Okay," the little girl replied, "I think that Dad wants to

kiss you in private." Peggy laughed as she went into Candi's bedroom and lay on the bed after turning on the TV.

It didn't take long before the girl was fast asleep. Candi covered her and closed the bedroom door.

"I adore her, Joe," Candi said as she returned to the couch and put her arms around Joe and kissed him. After putting her head on his shoulder, she told him about what Paul had said to her.

"Candi, you're probably worrying about nothing. I know that he's smart enough to realize that you're green but a gem. He was probably so worried abut you that he couldn't think straight."

She didn't say anything. She just put her head down on his breast and nuzzled his neck. After a few minutes, she said, "You're so nice, Joe. I love it when I'm snuggled against you."

He lifted up her head and kissed her. She put her head down again next to his shoulder and whispered, "Can we just sit here quietly for a few minutes?"

Joe nodded and began stroking her hair. She was almost asleep in his arms when Pam's car drove into the driveway.

CHAPTER 18

———

HEARING PAM'S CAR DRIVE UP broke the spell as both Candi and Joe went to the front door and waved to her. Pam went into her apartment because, as she said, "I'm bushed. That Phoenix traffic wears a person out."

"Well Candi, I better get going, too. Peggy and I both have to go to school tomorrow." Joe went in and brought Peggy out in his arms while Candi opened the back door of the car so Joe could put the sleeping youngster on the seat without waking her.

"Good night, Joe. It's been quite a day for me. I'm bushed too, and I didn't even have the excuse of Phoenix traffic." Candi found that she was indeed bushed because as soon as her head hit the pillow, she fell into a deep dreamless sleep.

When her alarm went off, Candi woke up and momentarily forgot the awful day she had yesterday. After taking her shower and preparing coffee, she went over to Pam's to find out what she had done in Phoenix. "Good morning, Pam. I've got a fresh pot of coffee brewing. Do you want to come over after you get dressed?" In an imploring voice, she begged, "Please do. I need some good advice, so please come over. Please come, Pam. It's very important."

Pam looked up from reading the paper and asked, "Did you see the paper this morning, Candi?"

"Not yet. Why? Is there something interesting in it?"

"There's an article about you on the second page. There's even a picture of you holding a big black dog."

"Oh, my God! Paul said he was going to write the report. He didn't say that he was going to call the press in." This is horrible! Can I read it?" She sat down with the paper while Pam passed her a cup of coffee.

After reading the small story beneath her picture, Candi knew that Paul had nothing to do with it. A spectator at the fire had taken the picture and called the paper after she and Paul left.

"What am I going to do, Pam? I know I'll be fired after the sheriff reads this and Paul's report."

"Why do you say that, Candi? It looks to me that you are a bit of a hero."

"No, I'm not. Paul called me a bitch. Actually he called me a stupid bitch. Oh, he softened it a bit when he saw me crying, but he still believes that I'm a stupid bitch, and I know that Clarence will too." Candi told Pam what had happened at the fire. Her version wasn't much different from the newspaper's, but she told of the flames and smoke and how she was affected by the burning rooms.

When she finished telling the story, Pam laughed and said, "It wasn't a very smart thing to do, but sometimes we do things without thinking it through. I think everything will be okay."

"Should I even go to work today?"

"I know you should. Remember the Shakespeare thing when he said 'The coward dies a thousand deaths. The valiant taste of death but once.' If you want me to go with you to work and try to explain what happened, I will."

"Thanks, friend, but I guess I've got to face the music alone. I remember the discussion we had about those lines from Shakespeare in Mrs. Fitzgerald's class when we were sophomores. I'll face the music alone and try to practice what Shakespeare said."

While drinking another cup of coffee, Pam heard her friend get into her car and head for the Pima sheriff's car park. *I hope she comes out okay. I want her to stay on the force and be my neighbor.*

When Candi drove up to the gate, the gatekeeper said, "I have a message for you. You're to report directly to the main headquarters as soon as possible. I was told to give you that message as soon as you came in."

Maybe I should have taken Pam up on her offer to come with me, Candi thought. Turning around and going to headquarters, Candi thought, *Well, I guess this tears it! I'll probably have to turn in my equipment and leave. Why else do I have to report there this morning?*

She was told by the clerk at the desk to report to Sheriff Dempsey's private office on the top floor. Candi looked closely at his face to see if she could get some hint from his facial expression. However, the clerk's expression remained bland.

Another clerk upstairs said, "Go right in, Deputy. The sheriff is expecting you." At this point, she considered just turning around and heading home.

As she entered, the sheriff got up from behind his desk. He was dressed semi-casually in a green shirt with a bolo tie around his collar. His dress pants were sharply pressed and his smile was big and welcoming. "Come in, Deputy, and have a seat." The sheriff came around and helped her to sit almost like a knight would for his lady. After Candi was seated, Sheriff Dempsey went back to his own chair and picked up the morning's <u>Arizona Star</u>. "Did you read the article about you in this morning's paper?"

"Yes, Sir, I did. I'm very sorry about that incident. I guess you also read Deputy Tallman's report."

"I did," replied the sheriff with a smile. "I guess we weren't wrong when we made you the honor grad at the academy. This kind of publicity helps the department. It lets the public see that we serve and protect."

Does he mean that? Now I'm really off balance. "Thank you, Sir. But I believe like Deputy Tallman said, it was extremely stupid of me, but I did it without thinking. I guess it was a big mistake. It probably was all in Paul's— I mean Deputy Tallman's report."

The sheriff called to his secretary, "Joan, would you have Deputy Tallman come to my office ASAP."

"Candi—may I call you Candi?"

"Yes, Sir."

"Deputy Tallman's report had nothing but praise for your conduct. He said it was the bravest and most honorable thing that he had ever witnessed. If it was up to him, he'd put you up for a medal of some sort, and Tallman's evaluations seldom offer such glowing words—at least they never did before."

"Sir, he said that I was stupid, and I certainly was."

"Paul told me about shouting at you and making you cry. He told me that he lost his temper for awhile because he was afraid that you'd be killed."

Candi rose as Deputy Tallman came into the room. He, too, was wearing a big smile as he greeted Candi, "I guess the sheriff told you about the next step in your training, Deputy."

"Not yet, Paul," the sheriff said. "I was saving that for when you came in." He turned to Candi and said, "Paul thinks, and I agree, that you should go to additional training in Phoenix. Their sessions are a bit harder, but all the detectives on our force have to have that training on their record. He'll need it because very soon, he'll be promoted to Detective." The sheriff looked straight at Candi, but he pointed at Paul.

It took quite a bit of willpower for Candi to <u>not</u> go around the sheriff's desk and hug both of the two grinning men.

CHAPTER 19

———✦———

WHILE THEY WERE LINGERING OVER a fast food meal at a nearby Taco Bell, Pam continued to laugh, "I can't get over the fact that you went to work this morning expecting to get fired and, instead, you get put in line for a promotion." Pam laughed loudly as she gripped Candi's hand.

"I can't get over it either. Sheriff Dempsey appears to be a very nice guy with a good sense of humor. He put me at ease when I went to his office because of his smile. His job likely requires that he needs a good sense of humor. It's probably as important to him as it is to teachers."

"He is a nice guy, but he usually makes someone work at least three years before sending them to detective school. You may be the first rookie so honored but don't let it go to your head. There are still a lot of bumps that go with your job."

"You said that you went up there last year and are near the top of the list to become a detective. How long was it before you were selected?"

"It was over three years. Tallman is right at the top."

"Yeah, I know that. He's the one taking me up there. The sheriff said he's going in for a refresher course and that he'll become a detective when he comes back from Phoenix."

"Remember, Candi, that I told you that he was tough, but fair. It took quite a man to admit that he treated you so badly yesterday."

Candi responded, "These days most of us tend to blame someone else for our mistakes. I don't care much for people who always say, 'It's not my fault.'"

Pam laughed again, "Now that Sheriff Dempsey gave you the whole weekend off with pay, what are you going to do with it?"

"First of all, I want to get up early so I can see you off to work and laugh as you get into your car."

"And after you stop laughing at me, what are you going to do?"

"I'm going to ask Joe if I can have Peggy for the whole weekend. If he says it's okay, we're going to the mall to bookstores, movies and kids dress shops. Then I'm going to take her to places like Mc Donald's and Long John Silvers only while I'm not making her read to me. I'm going to pretend that she's mine for the whole weekend. God, I wish that were true!"

"Don't worry about Joe. He'll jump at the chance to let you do things with Peggy. He knows that she loves you and wants to spend time with you."

"All three of us are going to do things together when you're off work. She wants to spend time with you, too."

"When Joe brought Peggy to Candi's apartment with a weekend supply of clothes, he said that he hoped Candi would enjoy her stay in Phoenix.

After two full days of being with Peggy, Candi knew that she had lost her heart to the little one. When Joe came on Sunday night to pick her up, she was sound asleep on Candi's lap. She had cried because Candi was going away for two weeks, but Candi assured her that Pam would spend the next weekend with her. Joe sat on the couch next to them and kissed them both. "Both of us will miss you while you're in Phoenix, and I hope your sheriff will realize what a gem he has and make you a detective like Nancy Drew was."

Before Joe left, Pam came over and made arrangements to have Peggy the next weekend. "Candi isn't the only one who wants to spoil her, Joe."

While Joe was carrying the sleeping girl out to his car, the phone rang. When Candi answered, she recognized Paul's husky voice immediately. "Meet me at the car storage area at about 7:00 in the morning. We have to check into the hotel and answer roll call before noon. The session starts with an introductory lunch."

"Okay, Deputy Tallman. I'll be there to meet you. I'm looking forward to meeting some law enforcement people from various places in Arizona. I certainly want to meet those from up north in Yavapai County since Prescott is the County seat, and it's where my roots are."

At the agreed on time, Candi met Tallman at the gate of

the car-park. After she parked her car, he came up to help her with some luggage and school supplies. When they had those stored in the county car, Paul said, "You drive. Are you nervous about the training?"

"No, not really, but I hope that you'll help me get over a few of my concerns since I haven't had a lot of experience."

What was Pam Henry's reaction when you told her about your session with the sheriff?" Paul smiled as he asked this.

"She really howled because I left for work that day fully expecting to be fired. And, Sir, what are your thoughts about being promoted?" These questions were asked as they drove out of Tucson on their way to Phoenix.

"I'm okay with it. I still get a kick out of patrol though. In that job, not many days are boring. There is always something new happening, such as a beautiful young girl going in and rescuing a dog." Candi looked over to him and caught him smiling. *He has as much of the dry sense of humor as Jim had, and his smile is almost exactly the same as Jim's. I hope that he doesn't tell too many people in the training program about rescuing the dog.*

"Can I ask you for a favor, Sir? I hope that what I did doesn't get bandied about while we're in school up there. I don't want deputies from across the state to know about the fire and dog."

"No, I won't Candi. That will remain our private joke as long as you quit calling me Sir. My name is Paul."

CHAPTER 20

———◆———

WHEN THEY RETURNED TO THE parking lot at the Pima County Sheriff's headquarters, Candi was happy. However, because of the grueling two-week session, she was almost totally worn out. Paul parked his car near hers and helped put Candi's luggage into her car. While they were standing near her driver's side door, she said, "Thank you, Paul. It was an exciting two weeks, and you helped me over a lot of rough spots." She moved into his arms and kissed him very gently.

He returned the kiss and whispered, "Candi, I've grown very fond of you. I hope that you have developed some fondness for me."

"I have, Paul, and I hope that we can see each other often in spite of your promotion to detective." Her smile was very sincere.

"I'm not a detective yet, Candi. Even if the sheriff makes me one, I hope we can continue our friendship." As he finished speaking, he kissed her again after pulling her close.

"Well, I guess I have to go. Pam will want to know all

about our experiences in Phoenix." She kissed him lightly on the cheek and opened her car door and climbed in.

On the way to the apartment, she thought about the trip to the Phoenix school. *They worked us very hard trying to teach us so many things. I know that it takes a lot of experience to apply some of the lessons, but Paul and others will be there to help me.*

When she pulled into the driveway, Pam immediately burst out of her apartment and ran to her. After hugging each other and pulling Candi's luggage into her apartment, Candi saw that Pam had been busy preparing for her homecoming. The room was spotless, iced tea glasses were on the small tables, and the smell of something delicious was in the air.

"Well, Pal. Did you learn a lot in Phoenix?"

"I sure did. They crammed my brain with so much stuff there isn't much room left for anything else."

"Tell me about it, but first tell me how did you get along with Paul?"

"Pam, he treated me wonderfully. He was more of a companion than he was a mentor. We went out to dinner several times, and he was a perfect gentleman. Having dinner with him was almost like it was with Jim Mitchell."

"Then you're no longer a 'stupid bitch' in his eyes?"

"I guess not. He didn't tell anyone at the school about that. Changing the subject a bit, did you have fun with Peggy while I was gone?"

"We had a great time, and both she and Joe asked about you a lot. I'm to call him the minute you arrive home."

As they were drinking iced tea, Pam asked about some of the classes.

"They assured us that it takes time to be like Sherlock Holmes, but the classes were a start. I loved the classes in interrogation techniques. Boy they really know how to tell if a witness is telling the truth or not. I kinda wish I had that training as a teenager so I could tell whether or not a boy was telling me that he loved me and really meant it or was just lusting over me."

Pam laughed and said, "That training will serve you very well when you need it on patrol from now on. Did they teach you how to fingerprint and look closely around a crime scene?"

"Yes. Looking at a crime scene as closely as competent detectives do takes a lot of training and experience. It's true that a good cop can see things that many people would miss. There was a lot of game playing with the lessons. My lack of experience really showed in the games."

While they lingered over dinner and coffee, Pam could tell that Candi was totally worn out. Pam watched her close her eyes several times while almost dozing off. "Go to bed now Honey. I'll clean up here. You need to be well rested because Peggy will be here tomorrow. Joe had a tough time holding her off 'til then. She wanted to be here to welcome you home. That little one sure loves you. And remember that you have to return to work on Monday. Your vacation is over now. A patrol car is waiting for you. Remember that you'll be in it all by yourself now. You won't have Paul looking over your shoulder any more."

"I know," Candi smiled weakly. "But Paul told me that backup is always close by. He also warned me to call for backup before trying to act like a tough movie cop that distains getting any help."

CHAPTER 21

AFTER CANDI RETURNED FROM WORK, she took off her uniform and put on her Levis and an old, flowered blouse. She settled herself in the recliner and opened her new Lee Child mystery. *I wonder what's keeping Pam. I hope she didn't get hurt again.* Settling back with the book, she read about 30 pages and then began to **really** worry. She looked at her watch and thought, *I'll give her another half hour and then I'll go out and look for her and call headquarters to see if anyone there knows anything.*

As her deadline was approaching, the phone rang. While she reached for it, she hoped it wasn't the sheriff's office or a hospital calling to inform her that something bad had happened to Pam.

She was much relieved when she heard Pam's voice. Without even a greeting, she heard, "How was your shift today, Candi?" While framing an answer, she heard Pam laughing.

"Pam, you heard about my shift. You knew before you asked that I had a miserable day."

Pam's laughter stopped and then she responded, "I know about it because the boss told me. He was chuckling about it so I don't think you have anything to worry about because it's really not too serious. Tell me about it when I get there. I'm buying a new pair of shoes at the mall, so have some hot coffee ready. I believe our Thanksgiving dinner tomorrow won't be held out on the patio because it's so cold It'll probably snow."

Candi laughed, "Snow in Tucson! I doubt it. I'll tell you about my miserable day when you get here, so please hurry so I can get it off my chest."

As she was hanging up the phone, she heard a car stop in the driveway. *I hope that it isn't a salesman. I'm not in the mood for that today.*

Before the bell rang, Candi opened the door. "TIM! TIM MONAHAN! WHAT IN THE WORLD..."

Tim smiled and said, "Hello, Lieutenant, how the hell are you?"

Candi rushed into his arms and hugged and kissed him before either of them said anything more. Tim was dressed in his green Class A uniform. From his spit-shined shoes and gunny sergeant stripes to the globe and anchor pin on his cap, he looked like a Marine dressed for a battalion inspection.

"Come in, Tim, and get warm. I've got some fresh, hot

coffee made." She pulled him in by pushing with her right arm that was still wrapped around his waist.

"What brought you to Tucson, Tim?"

"Lieutenant, I was transferred into your old outfit, and now I'm assigned to the recruiting office here. I sure wanted to see you, so Colonel Kincaid gave me your address. I just pulled into town yesterday. Is it true that you're with the sheriff's office here?"

"Yes, I am. Sit there and I'll get us a cup of coffee. My next door neighbor 'ordered' me to have a cup ready for her when she comes home. She's at the mall shopping."

While drinking coffee, they talked about many things. Candi asked about her friends and acquaintances still at Pendleton. "How's the Colonel these days?" she asked with a smile.

"He's as tough as ever, but he told me that he misses you and that he's coming to Tucson when he gets things squared away in the battalion."

"He'll probably never get that done to his satisfaction. I hope that he...Oh, I bet that's Pam now. Do you remember her? She was with me when I came to Pendleton to get my release last spring."

Tim smiled, "I sure do. I never forget a pretty girl."

Pam opened the door and rushed in. "Candi, how do you..." as she pointed to her new shoes. After noticing Tim, she stopped and looked at him waiting for Candi to introduce him.

"Pam, this is Tim Monahan. You met him when we went to Pendleton to get my release. He was the bartender in the O Club then."

Pam's face reddened as she remembered meeting him. *I told Candi that I thought he was very good looking. He's still as handsome as I remember.*

"Yes, I remember you, Tim. Are you on leave?"

Tim smiled at her, "I'm stationed here now. I'm at the recruiting office on Broadway."

"Tim, we're going out for Mexican food. I hope that you'll join us, but before we go can you give us about five minutes alone? I need to discuss something with Candi. It's sheriff's business."

"I'd love to have dinner with you ladies, and I'll go out on the patio and drink my coffee there."

After refilling his cup, Tim went out and sat on one of the comfortable patio chairs.

Pam pulled Candi down to the couch and held onto her arms. "Okay, tell me what happened between you and Sergeant Malone."

Chuckling, Candi started, "I was patrolling in that beautiful area near the Arabian farm out on Speedway. I parked near the stables at the bottom of a hill because speeders often put their cars into overdrive and fly down that hill. I don't want them to hit any horseback riders from the ranches around there. After a while, I got a little bored and didn't immediately pick up on a car going about 30 miles over the limit. That was Malone's car. She came back and parked across the street from me and charged over to my car. When I rolled down my window, she started screaming. 'DEPUTY ADAMS, WERE YOU ASLEEP JUST NOW? I CAME DOWN THAT HILL WAY OVER THE LIMIT IN A CAR WITHOUT A LICENSE PLATE OR TAIL LIGHTS. I KNOW I DIDN'T HAVE THEM ON THE CAR BECAUSE THEY WERE ON THE FRONT SEAT WITH ME.

'I'm sorry, Sergeant, I must have been day-dreaming for a minute or two when you came by.' I said sheepishly.

'I'm writing you up! You should know better than to day-dream while you're on duty. I'm also going to mention this to Paul Tallman since he's always bragging about you.'

I kinda hoped that she'd give me a break with only a warning, but she didn't."

Pam laughed, "She doesn't give breaks. She once wrote up her monitor when he was going only about 10 miles over the speed limit. Hank Williams still is a bit miffed about that."

Candi laughed, "I guess she does her job well. She probably keeps everyone on the ball, but I'm embarrassed about her catching me. What did Clarence Dempsey say?"

"He just laughed about it and said, 'I guess Candi screws up sometimes—like all of us do.' I know it's a little embarrassing, but keep your chin up. Now let's get that good-looking sergeant out of the cold and feed him a little good Mex food."

"Maybe we should call Joe and Peggy, and all of us go together. I want to have Peggy meet and *discuss* things with a real Marine. She'll be excited about meeting one, and I hope that you'll help him out a little when she wraps him around her little finger."

"Yeah, I'll do that so you and Joe can laugh at us. But, Candi, he's very nice looking. Is he married?"

"No, Pam, he's not. Do you want me to put in a good word for you?"

"Just be subtle about it."

"I will, but there's one drawback in dating a Jarhead: You have to stand up every time you hear the Marine's Hymn. If you don't, he'll pick you up bodily."

CHAPTER 22

WHEN THEY ALL RETURNED TO the apartment complex, they went into Candi's apartment to have a final cup of coffee. The living room was warm and inviting since they were a bit chilled after leaving the warmth of Candi's car. While Pam and Candi were fixing the coffee and cookie plate, Peggy continued bombarding Tim with questions about the Marines. Tim, who almost immediately fell for the little girl, answered her questions patiently with a smile playing about his lips. She huddled close to him on the couch asking about his uniform, ribbons, pins and buttons. Every now and then Joe would try to stop her torrent of questions but with no success. When Pam came out of the kitchen with a plate of cookies, the torrent was momentarily stopped as Peggy bit into a cookie and sipped a Pepsi.

When Candi's grandmother clock chimed that it was 9:00 pm, Pam said that she had to get up early in the morning to work a half day, Tim rose, "Pam may I see you to your door?"

"Sure, Tim, I'd like that. I know I'll be safe with a Marine escort."

"I think we'd better go as well. Peggy has to get up early to go Christmas shopping with her grandmother."

After Joe and Peggy left, Candi decided to sit up and read while she waited for Tim's car to leave. *Wow! He's been over there for over 30 minutes. I guess they're getting acquainted. I think Pam likes him—at least she acted like she did.*

After another 30 minutes of waiting, she heard Tim's car leave the driveway. She smiled and thought *I'll bet Pam will come over with a report.* She was right. Pam came over almost immediately wearing a large smile.

"Tim seems to be a very nice guy, Candi. Do you think so?"

"He's very nice, and the question is: do <u>you</u> like him? You guys talked for a long time. Anything I should know about you and him?"

"I'm going to help him find an apartment Saturday. Meanwhile I invited him to Thanksgiving dinner. Is that okay with you?"

"I'd be surprised if you didn't. Little Peggy adores him already. I know it's none of my business, but did you two do a little smooching?"

Pam's face gained a little color. "Yes, we did a little of that. At first, he gave me a 'gentleman's peck,' but I liked it so much, I returned it with interest. I could fall for that guy!

I'm glad that you and he were friends when you were in the Corps."

Candi laughed and hugged her friend. "I hope, Pam, that you and he get together. He treated me wonderfully the day Jim was killed. He was ready to punch out an officer who made a wisecrack about Jim and me."

The Thanksgiving dinner was a splendid affair even though it was indoors because of the cold. Grandmother Martha praised the girls' cooking in addition to bringing a rhubarb pie. Candi noticed that Pam and Tim held hands when they thought nobody was looking. After dinner, Peggy insisted that Tim tell a few stories about life in the Corps while she sat on his lap.

The next morning, Candi went again to the Arabian farms and parked in the same spot she was in when Malone caught her daydreaming. *I know she'll come down the hill again in a different car hoping to catch me napping again.* She was very alert today, and the drivers who used the road seemed to sense her interest and obeyed the speed limits especially when they noticed her patrol car parked by the side of the road.

Her attention was drawn away from the traffic when she heard a faint scream that got louder as a horseman approached the fence that enclosed the pasture. The horse was galloping very fast. The screaming continued as the rider came close to the fence. "HELP ME, PLEASE! I'VE BEEN SHOT AND THEYRE STEALING MY ARABIANS!"

Candi ran across the street and watched the woman fall

from the horse still shouting for help. Candi noticed she was bleeding from her shoulder. She climbed through the barbed-wire fence and ran to help the woman. "Never mind me. I'll be okay, but please stop them. My best horses are being loaded into their trailer! They're stealing them!"

After she ran back to her patrol car and radioed for backup, she drove to the farm's driveway and whipped her car through the gate. She parked it so that it effectively blocked the gate. Then she saw a truck with a horse-trailer coming toward her. While she listened for sirens coming down the road in the distance, the truck slowed as it came close to her car. She opened the door and was getting out when she heard a gunshot. She felt immediate pain as she was knocked back into the car. Terrified that she'd been mortally wounded, she pulled her weapon from its holster and turned her body around so she could see the stopped truck and horse trailer. Another shot rang out and a bullet zinged by her head and shattered her window. She fired back blindly and without any hope of hitting anything but, perhaps her shot might scare the two men.

Just then a car pulled into the driveway. A woman's voice shouted, "DEPUTY, ARE YOU ALRIGHT?" The voice came from the other side of her car.

"PLEASE DUCK, SERGEANT MALONE, THEY'RE SHOOTING AT US!"

Malone's gun sounded while the sergeant shouted, "PLEASE TELL ME, CANDI, ARE YOU HURT?"

"A bullet hit my vest. I don't think I'm hurt seriously, but I'm sure scared!"

Another car arrived with the siren screaming. Candi watched as the two men abandoned the truck and started running across a nearby field. A male voice shouted, "ARE YOU TWO ALRIGHT?"

Malone shouted, "THEY'RE RUNNING ACROSS THAT FIELD. TRY TO CATCH THEM WHILE I SEE TO THIS WOUNDED OFFICER!"

Dorothy Malone came over to the driver's side of the patrol car and reached in touching Candi to assure her that the danger was nearly over. Malone asked softly, "Are you bleeding anywhere? Will it be okay if I get you to sit up?" Candi tried to pull herself up and with Malone's help, sat up. Her gun was still in her hand.

"Just sit still, Adams. The ambulance and EMTs are not far away." Malone noticed a bullet had pierced Candi's blouse and probably still rested in her vest.

"Mrs. Riddle got hit. Please send help to her when they arrive. She's over there," Candi pleaded while pointing to the fence in back of her car.

"Mrs. Riddle is being attended to now. But, dammit, tell me if you need them to look you over."

"I don't think so. I'm more scared than hurt."

"I was scared, too, Candi." Malone reached in and put her arms around the deputy. "You were very brave today, Deputy, and besides you stopped a couple of horse thieves. That took some quick thinking."

In a few minutes, Paul Tallman and another officer returned with two men who had their arms handcuffed behind them. They both looked to be in their 20s and were very scruffy looking.

Paul said, "Malone, get on the horn and tell them that all is secure here. We'll take these sons of bitches in."

As Malone left to deliver the message, Paul looked in and hugged Candi. "My God, you gave me a scare. I'll drive you in and get someone to drive my car. George can handle our two prisoners"

In a moment he climbed in and pushed Candi gently over after he was seated and turned the car around and he sped back to headquarters. He looked at her noticing that she was trembling and hanging onto his arm. "Paul, I've never been so terrified as I was when they were shooting at me."

"Malone told me that you fired back at them. That was the right thing to do. We all knew that you'd act bravely when the chips were down because Marines are used to small firefights. The sheriff will be happy about your actions and anxious to talk with you."

When they got to headquarters, she was examined by medical people and then stripped out of all her clothes. "We need this vest for evidence." Malone, who had just arrived, put a long gown over her. While buttoning the gown, she added, "Candi, I'm so sorry that I wrote you up the other day. I'll see that none of that gets on your record."

Sheriff Dempsey, along with a whole battery of detectives and reporters, made her repeat her story many times while they recorded it.

Malone handed her a cell phone. "Call Pam Henry. She might think that you're dead."

When Pam answered the phone, Candi said, "Pam, I'm okay. I got shot at today, but I'm fine. The vest worked perfectly. I'm coming home soon with my friend Dorothy Malone." She smiled as she looked at Malone who was nodding and also smiling.

CHAPTER 23

———◆———

WHEN DOROTHY AND CANDI REACHED her apartment, they didn't have time to get out of the car because they were met by Pam. She jerked open the passenger door before Candi had released her seat belt. "ARE YOU ALRIGHT? SHOULD YOU GO TO A HOSPITAL?"

"No, Pam. I'm okay." As she started to crawl out of the car, Pam literally lifted her off the seat and hugged her tightly.

"My God! The sheriff called a few minutes ago telling me what happened out there. You got into a gunfight! Are you sure that you're completely okay? Let Dorothy and I help you into your place."

"Please, Pam, let me walk. I'm really not hurt—just a little sore where the bullet hit the vest."

"I called Joe at school. He's coming right over."

"You didn't tell him that I got shot, did you?"

"Yes, but I told him that you called and said that you weren't wounded."

Dorothy cut in, "Pam, she's fine. We took all her clothes

143

off including her bra to examine her. The vest, bra and blouse will be used as evidence. Before her boyfriend comes, let's let her get dressed—at least put on her underwear. On second thought, maybe we should leave her like she is. That may give her boyfriend a thrill."

For the first time since the sheriff called, Pam laughed. "I guess we better let her get dressed. He should be here in a minute or two."

Just then a car squealed to a stop in the driveway and Joe came in looking around.

Pam spoke up breaking the silence. "She's in the bedroom putting on fresh underwear and a dress. She'll be out in a moment, and she's fine. Have you met Dorothy Malone? She's the deputy who helped Candi this afternoon."

Dorothy and Joe shook hands while Pam started the coffee brewing.

Joe paced back and forth nervously until Candi came out of the bedroom fully dressed. He rushed over to her and smothered her in his arms. Realizing that she was okay, Joe whispered, "I guess you know now how Wyatt Earp felt at the OK Corral in Tombstone. Did you shoot anyone?"

"I'm no Annie Oakley, Joe. I missed by at least a half mile, but I scared them. They knew that they shouldn't mess with a woman with a gun." He kissed her several times before he released her.

"I'm sure glad that Dorothy came when she did. She was the one that scared them away—not me."

The four of them talked for over an hour before they drove to the nearest Taco Bell and had a small dinner.

Two days later Candi was shifted to the 4 to 11 shift, but patrolled in the same area where the gunfight had occurred. Mrs. Riddle often came out with fresh doughnuts and hot coffee. "Can I do more for you, Candi? You saved my beautiful Arabians?" Agnes Riddle carried the tray out in spite of having her right arm in a sling. Often, they shared the doughnuts and coffee with Dorothy when she stopped and sat with Candi.

One night about two weeks after the "Arabian" incident, Candi's radio informed her that a kidnapping had taken place in a Safeway parking lot in Tucson. Since it was after dark, the sheriff's office had only a partial plate, and witnesses were "almost" sure that the car was a green Dodge. While she was writing down the description, a car zipped by her followed closely by a sheriff's patrol car with siren screeching. Recognizing Joan's voice on her radio, she heard, "I'm in pursuit of a car that looks like the one the kidnapper used. All cars in the vicinity attempt to block the road at Houghton and Speedway. He's heading south on the road near the county line."

Candi did a snappy U-turn and followed the two speeding cars. As she came down a small hill, Candi saw a patrol car parked up against another car. When she stopped, Candi heard Joan screaming into her radio, "COME TO MILE POST 28. I'VE BEEN HIT! THE SUSPECT IS ON FOOT

NOW. I THINK THE KID IS SAFE BECAUSE I HEAR CRYING."

Candi rushed to the patrol car and noted Joan's bleeding leg. "I've called for help, Joan. Which way did he go?"

"Check on the kid in the back seat first, Candi. He headed for that barn across the road."

After checking on the boy who appeared to be terrified but okay, Candi followed Joan's instructions and set off in the direction of the barn with her weapon in hand. *Pulling guns out is getting to be a habit.* Since the night was very dark with no moonlight, she found following a trail was difficult.

When she reached the barn, she thought she heard a sound coming from inside near the loft. Tightening her grip on her pistol, she crept up to the small entrance door as soundlessly as she could while listening for another sound of movement. "COME DOWN WITH YOUR HANDS IN PLAIN SIGHT. YOU CAN'T ESCAPE. DO YOU HEAR THOSE SIRENS?" She waited cautiously for any noise, but heard none. *They trained me to wait for backup in these situations. I kinda wish I had followed their advice.*

She turned momentarily to see two deputies heading her way. When she turned, she saw in her peripheral vision a stick heading her way just before she was hit and fell stunned to the ground. The gun fell out of her hand, but she regained full consciousness moments later hearing gunfire from within the barn. After searching for her gun in the dark, she stood up and crept through the door. As she looked up she saw a man coming down a ladder toward two deputies holding guns at the ready. When the man was on the ground, he put up his hands which were quickly handcuffed by one of the big deputies. The other turned around and spoke to Candi, "We got him, Deputy." He smiled as she came close to him, "You can put your gun away, Adams. Now let's take him down the hill to check on Parmenter and get this bastard locked up."

When they came out of the bushes, they saw several cars parked nearby including an emergency ambulance. Candi ran forward to see two EMTs putting a tight bandage on Joan's leg. Rushing up to her, Candi asked, "Is she going to be alright? How do you feel Joan? We caught the guy who shot you and kidnapped the child."

Joan smiled through her pain, "I heard you got whacked with a pitchfork handle. How do YOU feel? I'll bet you'll have a lump on your head and a headache in the morning."

Candi smiled, "Only a small headache but no lump so far. I'm going to call Louise and go to the hospital with you. One of the EMTs insists that I go to be checked out." She smiled and added, "I suppose you'll want the day off tomorrow." Candi laughed and kissed her on the brow and held her hands while the EMTs loaded her on a small gurney to load her into the ambulance.

Before the ambulance started, Joan asked, "Is the kid alright? Is he the one that was kidnapped tonight?"

Deputy Mathews came forward then and answered, "The kid is fine—just scared. He's the one that was kidnapped. I guess the sheriff will probably have to take us out to dinner after you get on you feet, Parmenter." All the men laughed and started naming various restaurants that were excellent but expensive.

As the ambulance whizzed away, another patrol car came up and stopped. Louise Barrow came out and embraced Candi. "Let's ask the sheriff if we can sit in the hospital with Joan. We can't have one of the *three musketeers* alone in a dreary hospital room, can we?"

CHAPTER 24

———

SEVERAL DEPUTIES JOINED LOUISE AND Candi in the hospital waiting room. While there was concern about Joan, they covered it up by laughing and joking with each other. The men enjoyed walking up to Candi looking at her head and chuckling. She had been examined by a staff doctor and given a cold compress to reduce the swelling of a bump above her right ear.

After the wait, which seemed interminable, a doctor came out and said, "We're keeping Deputy Parmenter overnight. She's fine. The bullet just grazed her thigh, but we want to be sure she stops bleeding. She should be back at work in a few days."

When Louise and Candi walked out of the hospital, assured that Joan would be okay, they went to Louise's car and started for home. Although it was late, Louise came into Candi's apartment with her and Candi brewed a pot of coffee. They talked until shortly after 11 pm when Pam came in. "I saw all the lights on, so I knew that you guys were up and about," Pam said on entering. "Is there another cup of coffee in the pot?"

The three sat around the kitchen table until well after midnight before both Pam and Louise went home. However, Pam wouldn't budge until she got all the details of the night's patrol. She carefully examined Candi's bump while laughing.

Around 10 am the next morning, Pam came over. "The sheriff just called and wanted to know about your head. He wondered if you wanted the day off to recuperate. I told him I'd ask. How do you feel about working tonight?"

"I'm fine, Pam. Assure the sheriff that I'll go to work today. But what are you going to do with your day off?"

"Tim is coming over and we're going to a movie and dinner."

Candi smiled playfully, "You two are seeing a lot of each other. Is it getting serious?"

Turning serious, Pam answered, "I think it is, Candi. I think he's wonderful. I'm so glad that he's stationed here. I asked him if he left a girlfriend back at Pendleton, and he said, 'A BAM and I had a few dates, but she told me to get lost just before I got transferred here. I think she was upset that I wanted to come to Tucson.' I asked him what a BAM was and he said that it stood for Beautiful American Marine."

Candi chortled and asked, "Did he tell you what BAM really stands for with most Marines?"

Pam turned a little red with a smile, "Yes, he did. It stands for Broad-Assed Marine, but I like the other definition best. You were a Beautiful American Marine—not the other. Come on; let's have an early lunch before you go to work. I'll phone the sheriff and tell him that you'll be on time for your four to eleven shift."

"How does my head look? I tried to cover my bump by combing my hair over it?"

Pam inspected her head and pronounced, "I can hardly see anything. I've always said that you had a hard head, Candi. That was certainly true in high school."

When she arrived at work, several deputies came over and did their own playful inspections. As they got into their patrol cars, Louise asked, "Can we have coffee again tonight after work? That is unless something keeps us at work until midnight or longer."

"Sure. I'll meet you at the car park shortly after eleven."

She regretted that her assignment was changed to the Nogales highway area because Mrs. Riddle wouldn't be there to supply hot coffee. Just as she was about to start patrolling some of the dirt roads that lead off the highway, she saw a car coming very fast toward her. It was coming from the Green Valley area and appeared to be weaving all over the highway.

Oh, oh! This guy is either too tired to drive or is too drunk. She started her car, made a quick U-turn, and began a chase. She radioed that she was in pursuit of a speeding car and gave the license number she had copied to the dispatcher.

The driver of the car she was following saw that he was being followed and turned quickly off the highway into a pecan tree grove in an effort to hide from the pursuing patrol car. But the driver lost control and his car fell into a bar ditch shortly after he left the highway.

Candi stopped just behind his rear bumper and radioed what happened and gave her location to the dispatcher.

She exited her car and walked carefully over to the driver's side of the damaged vehicle. "Roll your window down, please, Sir," she asked calmly but was prepared for any kind of trouble.

The driver, who appeared to be quite young, rolled down his window and said, "I'm sorry, officer. I made the corner too fast. Let me back up and I'll be on my way. I don't think my car is hurt much."

"Let me see your license and registration, please."

"Ah, er...I think I went off without them. They're at home in my wallet."

Beside the young man sat a huge older man. He reminded Candi of the movie she had seen once called <u>The Incredible Hulk</u> or a name something like that. *He must weigh over 300 pounds and is very mean looking.* Looking into the back seat, she saw two young girls, perhaps college age, sound asleep with their skirts pulled up showing their underwear. *Falling into that ditch should have awakened them.* "Sir, you in the passenger seat, reach back and rouse the girls. I want to talk to them."

The hulk reached back and shook both of them getting no response from either of the girls. *They're either stoned out of their mind or they might be dead.* "Rouse them again, Sir."

Again the hulk reached back while saying, "It's no use, Bitch. They're out of it. Too much brandy, I guess."

"Watch your language, Sir. Please let me see your ID."

"Fuck you, Bitch! Let's get out of here, Lloyd."

The young man named Lloyd, turned the key and started the motor while twisting the steering wheel trying to get out of the ditch.

Candi pulled her tazer out of her belt, "SIR, TURN OFF THE ENGINE IMMEDIATELY OR YOU'LL REGRET IT!"

The boy turned toward the hulk before stopping the engine. The big man opened the passenger door quickly shouting, "I'm going to fix you, Babe!"

Stepping away from the door, Candi shouted, "GET OUT OF THAT CAR WITH YOUR HANDS IN PLAIN SIGHT!" The boy saw the weapon in her hand and immediately opened the door. Coming from the front of the car, Candi saw the 300-pound brute bent low running toward her. She aimed and pulled the trigger on her tazer. The brute fell to the ground screaming and helpless. Still holding her weapon on the younger man, she walked over to the big man and put handcuffs on his wrists with his arms behind him.

To the younger man, she said, "Lean on the car with your hands up, Sir!" She walked over and patted him down. The terrified boy said, "Drugging the brandy was all Frank's idea, Ma'am. I didn't mean no harm. We was just going to…"

"Going to do what?"

"We was going to screw them and then leave them in a ditch in some park."

The boy stopped as he heard a siren coming down the highway. Almost immediately a patrol car with lights on was seen turning off the highway on the road where they were stopped.

Frank Mathews jumped out of his car and ran toward where Candi was standing holding her weapon on the younger man leaning against his car.

"Thanks for coming, Deputy Mathews. I have a drunk, under-aged driver and a monster who tried to overpower me. He's the one over there with his hands handcuffed behind his back. Hold these two, while I check on two girls in their backseat."

Upon examining the girls, Candi found them drugged, but alive. Frank's car was immediately followed by an ambulance. When the two men were loaded into the back of Frank's car and securely locked in, Frank came over saying, "Deputy Adams, you did a great job tonight. We checked on the car when you called in the license number. The car was stolen tonight in Cochise County. Their dispatcher told me that they had identified the thieves for stealing the car and beating up a local cop near Douglas. That's why I was sent out as backup for you. The EMTs tell me that the girls will be okay in the morning. You heard the young man say that a pill was in their drink. I'm sure they'll thank you in the morning after they wake up."

Both deputies then searched the car and found a bottle containing over 20 tablets of ecstasy and some packets of white powder.

When she arrived home with Louise, they found Pam and Tim in a tight embrace in Pam's apartment. Still being totally awake from her experience with the hulk and his younger crony, Candi suggested that they all go to IHOP for either a late dinner or an early breakfast. When they arrived at the restaurant, Candi was somewhat calmed down, but was anxious to share the story with Tim and Pam.

"My Gosh! You took down two of them single handedly! I'm so proud of you, I could bust." Pam beamed.

"All in a day's—I mean night's work," smiled Candi.

Chapter 25

"Hi, Candi," Pam smiled while holding a glass of sun tea. She was sitting on Candi's recliner reading a magazine when Candi arrived. "How was your patrol today?"

"Just routine, thank God!" Candi responded as she began taking off her belt and vest. "I picked a drunk out of a ditch and almost strained my back lifting him into the back seat. Not only was he overweight, but he was really out of it. The best part was that both he and the car he was driving were in the ditch. He had no ID on him so I checked the glove box. To my surprise, it turned out to be a stolen car, so he went to jail instead of the drunk tank. How was your day?"

"Another boring, routine day, but they're the kind we love. By the way, you have a message on your landline."

"Please pour me a glass of that tea while I find out who called."

Pam went into the kitchen while Candi pressed the message button on her phone.

"Hi, girls, this is Joe. Peggy and I are going up north. I got a call from the president's office at NAU. I need to have an interview in the morning. We're taking Grandma Martha up with us because she wants to see a friend in Cottonwood whom she hasn't seen in a few years. They plan to explore there for possible retirement apartments for each of them. I'll leave Peggy with her while I go to Flagstaff in the morning. You know that I applied for a job there in the English department a few months ago, and I'm one of the finalists. I don't know much about it yet, but it's a chance to nearly double my salary. I'll call when we return tomorrow evening. Wish me luck."

Both Pam and Candi stood there stunned by Joe's message. "I didn't know that he had applied at NAU," Candi said in a perplexed voice. "Did you?"

"No, I didn't. He must have applied before we knew him or he would have at least mentioned it."

Candi responded, "Once he did say that he'd like to teach in college someday, but I thought he was just dreaming about it."

Pam took a swallow of her tea and responded. "If Grandma Martha goes to Cottonwood and Joe goes to Flag, we'll not be able to see much of Peggy in the future."

Chuckling a bit, Candi said, "I kinda hope that Joe changes his mind or they pick someone else because of Peggy. Also, as you know, I'm very fond of Joe. I know it's love. If both of them go out of my life, I don't know what I'd do." The chuckle faded and tears welled up in her eyes.

"I know you love him. I'm with you in hoping he stays here, but he should go where he feels happier. Do you love him so much that you'd quit your job here to go to Flagstaff with him?"

"Pam, I think I'd walk through hell if he was at my side. But he never asked me if I'd go with him if he left Tucson. I feel just like I did with Jim. I'm sure that if Joe were to ask me to go with him Sheriff Dempsey would understand. Maybe he could recommend me to the sheriff at Coconino County."

"Would Joe let you continue as a deputy there? He doesn't like you working here."

"Well," Candi said," I think Joe would leave that decision up to me, but we'd better wait to see if Joe gets the job and if he wants me to go with him."

Both of them silently sat together on the couch and drank their tea.

While on patrol the next day, Candi was almost too busy thinking about Joe to pay a lot of attention to her duties. When she came into her apartment after her shift, she looked anxiously at the phone to see if any message was from Joe. Pam came in shortly asking, "Is there any news?"

"No, nothing. Do you want a glass of tea?"

"Sure, but I'd probably feel better with something stronger.

Can I have a brandy and soda instead, and maybe you should have one too."

Without thinking about dinner, both women just sat silently waiting for the phone to ring. Both sipped their brandies until just after 6:00 pm when the phone rang and both sat still momentarily hoping it was Joe to tell them that he didn't get the job.

At the third ring, Candi shook herself loose and picked it up. "Hello." Her voice came out slowly and a bit fearfully.

"Hi, Candi. Peggy and I'll be over in a few minutes, if it's okay. We'll drop Martha home first. I've got some good news."

"Okay, Joe." As Candi put the receiver down, she began to tear up.

"Pam, he said that he had good news. I know he got the job and will leave Tucson." She went over to Pam and sat down and put her head against Pam's shoulder.

"Candi, he loves you as much as you love him. Please stop crying and let's just hope for the best."

Later while Candi was still wiping her eyes, they heard Joe's car pull into the driveway. Pam held tightly to Candi's hand while waiting for the door to open. When it did, Peggy ran into the room to where Candi was sitting. "Candi, it snowed in Cottonwood, and I built a little snowman." She put her arms around Candi and reached up to kiss her. Noticing Candi's tears, she asked, "Candi, why were you crying?"

"Peggy, why don't we go to my apartment and make a

little fudge? I think that your dad probably wants to talk to Candi about the trip."

Pam went out of the open door with Peggy almost dancing while holding tightly to Pam's hand. They passed Joe as he was entering the apartment.

"Candi, you've been crying. What's the matter? Did something terrible happen at work again today?"

She went over to the couch and sat near him. "No, Joe. I guess that I just needed to cry a little. Women often need to do that. What's the news from Flag?"

"I was offered the job, and I said that I'd let them know if I'd take it on Monday. I think I've always wanted to teach in college ever since I was a student at Washington State."

"That's wonderful, Joe. You'll get your dream to come true."

"While we were driving home, I knew that going to college wasn't what I wanted most."

Candi interrupted, "What was that, Joe?"

"It's you!"

Joe, I don't understand…"

"Candi, I spent the four hours driving home composing a speech I wanted you to hear. I had it all memorized, but when I saw you'd been crying just now, I lost it, but let me try…"

"Joe…"

"Please, Candi. Let me try. You know that I love you very much. When Rosemary was killed, I never thought that anyone could take her place in my heart. I kinda built a shield around it with only room for Peggy. But knowing you, that shield went away and you walked into my heart.' He reached for both of her hands and continued, "Please marry me if you feel a little love for me. I want us to be together always."

"Joe, do you know why I had been crying when you came in?"

"No, I don't but I thought it had to do with work. Please tell me."

"I was crying because I thought that you might NOT make that beautiful speech. I also thought I'd never love again after Jim, but then you walked into my life. I love you too, and I'd love to marry you and go with you anywhere you want to go. "

They both came together kissing and laughing.

"I didn't feel it was fair, but my best argument in the speech was that Peggy wants you to be her mother. I'm so glad that she will have a mom again, and it will be you."

As he spoke, both Pam and Peggy burst into the room with Peggy running to hug and kiss Candi. "I hoped that you would be my mother. I asked God to make you my mom. Pam told me that you wanted that too."

Joe rose from the couch and spoke through the laughter of Pam and Candi, "Let's all go to dinner to celebrate—on me. Pam, call Tim and tell him we're going to have a party and insist that he join us."